low diction
if you know what I mean

Of
This
New
World

The

John

Simmons

Short

Fiction

Award

University of

Iowa Press

Iowa City

Allegra Hyde

Of
This
New
World

University of Iowa Press, Iowa City 52242
Copyright © 2016 by Allegra Hyde
www.uiowapress.org
Printed in the United States of America

The University of Iowa Press is a member of Green Press
Initiative and is committed to preserving natural resources.
Printed on acid-free paper

Library of Congress Cataloging-in-Publication Data
Names: Hyde, Allegra, author.
Title: Of this new world / Allegra Hyde.
Other titles: Short stories. Selection
Description: Iowa City : University of Iowa Press, 2016. | Series: Iowa short fiction
award
Identifiers: LCCN 2016008377 | ISBN 978-1-60938-443-2 (pbk) |
ISBN 978-1-60938-444-9 (ebk)
Subjects: LCSH: Utopias—Fiction. | Psychological fiction. | BISAC: FICTION /
Short Stories (single author). | GSAFD: Science fiction.
Classification: LCC PS3608.Y365 A6 2016 | DDC 813/.6—dc23
LC record available at https://lccn.loc.gov/2016008377

For my family

"But first, whom shall we send

In search of this new world? whom shall we find

Sufficient? who shall tempt with wand'ring feet

The dark, unbottomed, infinite abyss . . .?"

—JOHN MILTON

Contents

In etymological terms, the word *utopia* means both "good place" and "no place"—a paradox by definition—and therefore best suited to the realm of imagination. This book, likewise, may have remained an idea if it weren't for lots of help along the way. I am sincerely grateful to the writing teachers who have given my work so much time and attention: Mike McNally, Melissa Pritchard, Pete Turchi, Matt Bell, Tara Ison, Jim Shepard, Andrea Barrett, and Karen Russell. Thank you also to the brilliant and generous friends I've made across many continents. Let's keep running into one another. To Alex: you're a dream and a half. To my family: I feel lucky to have been raised by people who believe writing is important—or at least "not making the world worse."

Lastly, I am grateful for the support I have received from the Virginia G. Piper Center for Creative Writing, the National University of Singapore, the San Miguel Writers Conference, Writing Workshops in Greece, the Swarthout Family, the Island School, Williams College, and most of all, from Happy Valley, where I learned that spelling didn't matter as long as I got the words out.

The stories in this collection have appeared in slightly different forms in the following publications: "The Future Consequences of Present Actions," the *Gettysburg Review*; "Delight®," *Black Warrior Review*; "Flowers for Prisoners," *Alaska Quarterly Review*; "After the Beginning," *Denver Quarterly*; "Shark Fishing," *New England Review*; "Americans on Mars!" *Passages North*; "Syndication," *Nashville Review*; "Bury Me," the *Missouri Review* and the *Pushcart Prize XL: The Best of the Small Presses*; "VFW Post 1492," the *McNeese Review*; "Ephemera," *Southwestern American Literature*; "Free Love," *Bellevue Literary Review*.

Of
This
New
World

After
the
Beginning

After the beginning, even seven days out, my husband still made me crazy.

We had been given a pile of sheepskins upon our expulsion—that was all. That and the promise of eternal suffering.

My husband seemed unable to get over this.

Seven days out, and by midmorning he still lay sprawled across the fleecy blankets lining our lean-to. I had built the lean-to; I had set pine boughs against a low branch to suggest some semblance of separation between the wilderness and us. A weak defense against new dangers (*Yes, I still remember when there was only one danger*), but a defense nonetheless.

By noon, though, the pine-boughs could not keep out the sun. Light jabbed between branches, waking my husband. He groaned and stretched his legs. His thigh muscles quivered.

"Put something on," I hissed, adjusting my own leafy apron.

He tugged a sheepskin across his lap and looked away, still unwilling to speak to me (*Yes, I remember disregarding that first danger*).

Even so, I told him I'd found a place to cultivate some food. I told him that without his labor we would never survive. I told him that he had to—he needed to—get up.

He still said nothing.

I decided to be good then: to feel shame and be bent by it.

My daydreaming made this difficult. I could not gather reeds or collect firewood or mend the lean-to without drifting into other places: to that lush ambrosial garden, the once warm cavern of my husband's embrace. All morning I swatted flies and images. To concentrate, I clutched tight to my guilt. I gave myself more chores. And yet, even as I wove reeds in the lacy shade of apple trees (*They were everywhere, those trees, growing wild and wormy like unfunny jokes*), I could not resist looking across the field to where my husband stood, head bowed. Lost in his thoughts.

"Gardens don't grow on their own," I called. A reminder, I suppose, that neither of us needed.

My husband stabbed a stick at the soil, ignoring me.

I gave up on weaving reeds and went back to fetching firewood.

All day my husband tilled the soil, sulkily. By late afternoon, his skin had turned red and raw from the sun. His flesh was glossed with sweat.

"At your rate," I said, "maybe we'll have something to eat in three years."

"Graah!" he yelled at last, throwing the stick down and striding into the forest.

Even as he disappeared, even as my own fingers bled from dryness and blisters, I dreamed. I thought about the intersection of our bodies, of shadows blooming in the sticky convergence of hip to hip.

My husband returned at nightfall, bruised, bee-stung, covered in mud. Empty-handed,

I wanted to laugh at the mess, the way we used to giggle at everything. There was a time when a bee sting would have been hilarious, even beautiful.

My husband slunk into the lean-to and curled up among sheep-skins, silent.

There were only apples to eat. We had been eating them raw for seven days. This must have been part of our punishment: to find ourselves nauseous from the sweet flesh, to start hating the snap of teeth through skin, the bite once wrongly desired. But there was nothing else to eat, so that night I mashed the fruit together and placed it on a flat rock near the fire.

"We should name this," I said, presenting the warm mush to my husband. Words, in those days, could still be plucked from the air. "How about . . ." I paused, awaiting the mouth-tingle of a new sound, ". . . how about 'pie'?"

He smiled—an expression I had not seen in days—and chewed slowly.

This was the first thing we had named since our expulsion.

I watched my husband, his face illuminated by our bonfire, his eyes tracing the arc of my collarbone, the curve of my breasts. The nakedness he'd only recently learned to see.

I will be good. I will feel shame and be bent by it.

That night we lay together on the pile of sheepskins, alone in a forest of shrieks and howls. I listened to the creatures outside—clawed and toothed—among which I'd once roamed freely. There were so many dangers now. So many clefts and cracks in the walls of our lean-to. So little we could do.

That night, our limbs entwined, my husband breathed softly, deeply.

And me: I dreamt of fields of grain and wicker baskets and paradise.

Shark
Fishing

There was a storm, a shipwreck. There were Puritans looking for a place to pray. A reef—serrated and rising from the sea—named the Devil's Backbone by those who outswam the drowning tug of hosiery and buckled boots, the swift darkness in a throatful of brine, who felt the soft footing of a sandy shore.

The island they named *Eleuthera,* a Greek word for freedom.

Then there was a cave like a yawning mouth: a home, high-ceilinged, acoustics of the finest church. A rocky pulpit—too perfect for coincidence—a sign to the Eleutherans. A gift from God. The island knelt before them, a blank surface of sea and sky, waiting to be given a past and a future.

This is that future: the locals call the island "Lutra," as if sun and salt could erode letters too. They fish from docks staggering rotten-legged into the sea, their bodies black against the horizon, like human hieroglyphics. And yet—how hard it is to read the meaning in their poses. To separate defiance from defeat. These children of children of children of slaves, shackled and shipped to an island named Freedom.

The locals, they speak too quick to understand sometimes, their voices like chiming bells. "Dats da ting," they tell me, dark arms lifting slack fishing lines. "Groupa gettin smalla an smalla."

Before long, the Eleutherans feared they'd failed their maker. The rye they'd planted hadn't come. Their few spades cracked and split. They sweated, starved, dug graves for their companions. Gripped scripture with cracked and bleeding hands.

AFFLICTION IS A BITTER ROOT, BUT IT BEARS THE SWEETEST FRUIT.

"Got 'em," says Nehemiah, reeling in a dripping fish, scales silver. He knifes the belly open, shows me a final rubied pulse. He looks relieved. Remorseful. "Only da old men do da dirty work now," he says, tossing fish guts off the dock. "Da kids, dey all gone."

The sun hangs low, hammocked by the afternoon.

The sea swallows a little more of the coast.

BUT IT BEARS THE SWEETEST FRUIT

The Eleutherans begged for help from northern churches, praised God when it arrived—bundled and blessed—on a charitably chartered vessel. They unpacked crates of sugar and salted pork; axes, hoes, and saws; they unpacked munitions and pewter spoons; beeswax candles, starched white linens, and silver sewing needles; they unpacked the makings, or so it seemed, of a bold new civilization.

To proffer thanks? The Eleutherans shipped ten tons of Braziletto timber back to Boston. The wood became precious anywhere but on the island. Red-grained, it was good for fabric dyes and violin bows. Its sale endowed Harvard University.

I am at the same university, hundreds of years later, in a room engorged with students. I am here to speak of Eleuthera—an island fragment in the spill of the Bahamas—to speak of Camp Hope, our work there, a new era of environmental innovation.

I have become like Braziletto: valuable elsewhere.

The students shift in their seats. Stare with cautious piety.

I shift too, hands braced against the podium, waiting for my words to settle into order, the ones that have ballooned and thickened, made me a new kind of evangelist.

"Thank you, I—"

But my words, I feel them crowded out.

"I—"

The Eleutherans. They wander through my mind as if they'd colonized that too.

Things disappeared on the island. The Eleutherans never met the Lucayans, a boatbuilding people who walked its beaches before them, who canoed between coves, gold-cheeked and sable-haired. Who disappeared, some years earlier, when the Spanish dropped anchor and enslaved them all.

The Lucayans: the goldest thing *Cristóbal Colón* could find.

The Eleutherans roamed all over their new home, discovering mounds of picked-out mussel shells, shards of palmetto ware. They found Lucayan axe heads, arrowheads, skulls—eye sockets spilling sand—in the place they'd come to call Preacher's Cave.

The Eleutherans discarded these scraps of the past.

Seated in front of my podium, a bone-pale girl peers into me as if through water.

You're imagining it.

Down, down, down through all the strata of civilization.

You're just nervous.

I've made this speech dozens of times—variations on an environmental homily, an ode to conservation—I've spoken without pause or hitch, without grasping for words, but now time dilates, my head throbs with the longings of ghosts.

You're—

Inside the airplane, inside the sky, window ovals opening into aquamarine—an ocean spread blank and blissful below—except for a few dark patches you realize later are the shadows of clouds. *The plane hovers there too: toy-sized and skimming the surface. And then, closer to land, sandbars swoop up white and dreamy, like spilt milk. There, Eleuthera. That skinny spit. That fishhook bathing. The toy plane glides over pink-pebbled beaches and acres of palm trees, above the square stamp of rooftops and swimming pools resigned to a viridescent shimmer. It dips to pineapple fields, bent and overgrown, to backhoes abandoned midpush in the dense coppice that jostles cinder-block settlements, right up to the tiny airport in Rock Sound—the only one left after Pan Am disappeared—and it feels as though you might disappear as well.*

I wound up at Camp Hope by luck.

Or fate.

In those days I didn't bother with distinctions: one minute I was in a single-bulb basement in Brooklyn, printing pamphlets on *Climate Justice in an Age of Corporate Tyranny*. The next, I was stepping onto the parched tarmac of the Eleutheran airport, about to work for a man I'd never met, wishing I still felt the reckless confidence I'd flaunted to friends back home.

Waiting on the tarmac: Mr. Roy Adams. My new boss and Camp Hope's founder, he was also—according to the rumors on the activist circuit—a former Navy SEAL turned born-again tree hugger, baptized in the warm waters of the Caribbean.

He wore aviators, a crew cut, and steel-toed boots.

Not my usual company. Not by a long shot.

"Let's go." Adams grabbed my duffel bag and chucked it into the back of a bug-smeared Jeep. Then he swung himself into the driver's side.

For a moment I considered refusing: catching the next plane back to New York. How could I work for a man who didn't even bother shaking hands? Having spent the last decade volunteering for Fieldcore—a loose collective of urban eco-activists, occasionally anarchic, always up in arms—I was used to group-think sessions that began with hugs and ended in drum circles, not two-syllable commands.

"Dawn?" said Adams. He was watching me through the Jeep's windshield, his posture relaxed, his gaze steady, as if I were an animal he'd already corralled.

I wanted out of that gaze, out of the sun's dizzying heat, and yet I thought of the offer Adams had made on the phone four weeks earlier. "Dawn," he'd said, "your work on that BP protest—impressive stuff—but don't you ever think of taking things further? Living the solution?"

Living the solution. Sure I'd imagined it—we all did at Field-core—we'd talk about getting a "chunk of land," starting an "eco-centered society," proving one could exist beyond the American SOP of morning commutes and disposable Starbucks cups.

But the talk had always stayed abstract. A hash-fumed fantasy.

That is, until Adams called and offered me a job.

"Camp Hope," he'd said, "will be part school, part eco–base camp. We're aiming to be a hundred percent self-sufficient within two years, with wind turbines, aquaculture, the whole deal. And we've already got a roster of students—or more specifically, their tuition—now we just need teachers. People who believe in sustainability. People like you."

People like you. Who was I except someone who'd always been willing to dream?

"Hot here," I said, sliding into the Jeep's passenger side. The vinyl seat burned the backs of my thighs, but I bit back a yelp, adding, "Barely fifty when I left New York."

Adams grunted, then rummaged in his pockets for keys.

It occurred to me, then, that he might have his own reservations. On the phone he'd said that I came "highly recommended," but he'd also repeated the need for "full-on commitment." That he needed "doers, not just dreamers. No wishy-washy hippie stuff." Apparently several recruits for his eco–dream team had already dropped out.

With my rumpled T-shirt and matted hair, I could hardly look inspiring.

Perhaps my ex-girlfriend—a lipsticked NYU professor with a penchant for "soft bohemian women"—had been right to smirk as she watched me pack. Perhaps she'd been right to remind me, in her creamy voice, that I'd never held a real job for more than a month.

I felt nauseated. Heat shimmered off the tarmac, blearing the tangle of trees and blossoms beyond. Adams revved the Jeep's engine. Unexpectedly, I smelled French fries.

"That biodiesel?" I asked, out of habit.

Adams turned to me, sunshine gilding his aviators so that for a moment he appeared both blinding and holy. Then he answered, "They said you were good," and stomped the accelerator, sending us careening toward Camp Hope.

So full of conviction, the Eleutherans had sold nearly everything before leaving England. Then they packed their remaining possessions—a few embroidered linens, the family's Geneva Bible—and sailed blind across an ocean as vast as an idea.

To Every Shareholder: liberty of conscience

To Every Shareholder: liberty of worship

To Every Shareholder: three hundred acres of land

My first eyeful of Camp Hope felt like a fever dream, a sight so gorgeous it hurt. Strung along a beach stood dormitories and classrooms, a dining hall and library—low breezy buildings, all freshly whitewashed—and beside them garden plots already flush with melon leaves, carrot tops, pole beans. Solar panels bowed to the sun. Wind turbines pirouetted in the breeze.

A citadel to sustainability.

"You weren't kidding," I breathed, standing beside Adams. "This *is* something."

Adams thrust his hands into his pockets, like an oversized boy trying to be modest. "It's getting there," he said, then paused. Nearby, several builders sat in the shade of leafy bananas.

"Are they local—?"

Adams ignored me, instead calling to the men, "Finished already?" as they scrambled upright. "Don't strain yourself, Dwain." Adams strode in among them, thumping the sweaty back of the slowest. "I'm in the market for more shark bait."

Dwain—or the man who'd been called Dwain—stiffened.

Adams released a gunshot laugh. "I'm just messing with you," he said, grinning until the others grinned with him.

Again I felt a wave of doubt, but there was little time to dwell. Adams had me meet the other faculty: in addition to a small platoon of biologists, he had recruited a trio of women fresh from liberal arts colleges, who looked competent and overeducated, and who—upon noting my cropped hair and cargo shorts—promptly informed me that they "loved Judith Butler." Then there was a gangly ex-Mormon named Charlie, who knew trigonometry and CPR. A busty scuba instructor named Jacquelle. Two silent Norwegian cooks, who vanished as soon as they were introduced. And me, presented as "a veteran environmental activist," a title that made me blush.

I didn't argue with it, though.

"In six days our students arrive," said Adams, as we gathered under palm trees for our inaugural faculty meeting. "Camp Hope, though, should be more than a school. Think of this place as our headquarters. The nerve center of an eco-revolution—not just here—everywhere. If we can end overfishing on Eleuthera, end the island's dependence on fossil fuels, the coastal-rape of mega resorts, we can be a model for the world to change."

With toes scrunched in sand, trade winds teasing our hair, all of us nodded—nearly *amened*—but Adams waved us quiet.

"And change is possible," he said, his voice tightening. "Look at me—look at who I was." He folded his muscled arms across his chest, again the Navy SEAL. "In Panama they asked me to blow up reefs, just to make extra harbor space. And I did. I blew them up."

He stared toward the setting sun, as if waiting for admonishment, some censure.

Only a demure slosh of seawater answered. The shy susurration of palm fronds.

"Now, though"—Adams's voice softened—"now, I protect them."

A week later, our first students tiptoed from a small metal plane, looking for someone to tell them what to do.

Nehemiah remembers when she came smiling off that plane: Princess Diana on her honeymoon. There were resorts on the island then, clinging to the coasts like barnacles. Coves full of yachts. Billy Jean King swatting balls across tennis courts. Music drifting from the bars.

Then there was a storm, resorts wrecked. Hurricane Andrew pummeled the island flat. After the storm, investors looked away. The big airport closed. No more tourists. No more jobs. Just empty afternoons, the bark of stray dogs.

"Mamma, she worked ina office," Nehemiah says, spitting off the dock. "And Papa, he worked in one nawta here."

I wasn't sure what to make of Camp Hope's students at first. There were thirty in total, all about fifteen years old, well-nourished, athletic—taking a semester sojourn from New England prep schools—the beautiful sons and daughters of bankers and doctors and politicians. Children of wealth. Adams needed their tuition, I knew, to keep Camp Hope afloat, but it disturbed me: serving the already privileged. Before classes began, I imagined myself being stern with them, yanking the silver spoons from their mouths. Giving them a bitter dose of reality.

I suppose I was jealous too. Or embarrassed. The students brought to mind my own scattershot upbringing—angsty and ugly—my mother's sigh of relief when I told her, at seventeen, that I was leaving for New York and never coming back.

And my father? Who knows what he thought.

The students, though, were a bright, cheery bunch. Hardworking. Despite my best efforts, I liked them. Nevertheless, when Adams asked for suggestions during a faculty meeting, I brought up the possibility of a scholarship fund. "For, you know, some diversity."

My proposal made Adams stand up and sigh. He paced the small office, then paused and pounded the table. A potted ficus jumped.

"Hell!" he said. "I'd love to elevate all humanity. But some ghetto baby isn't going to knock Exxon off its throne."

At "ghetto baby," the liberal arts girls looked as though they'd been Tasered. Charlie cupped his chin in his hand, brow furrowed. The biologists blinked. I leaned back in my chair, arms crossed, but Adams continued unperturbed.

"These kids, though—our kids—you get these kids hugging trees now, they'll be writing the laws later." His voice shifted, dropped lower. "You know what I mean?" He leaned against the table, looked right at me. "You ever change any laws, Dawn?"

The question made my face hot. I'd lain in front of bulldozers, graffitied the cars of CEOs, made hundreds of phone calls—all things that had felt meaningful at the time—but my answer to Adams's question? No.

"We get these kids on our side," he continued, "we'll have people with power on our side. We get them fighting our fight, we'll actually see some progress."

I didn't like the argument—its coldness and calculation—and yet in the days that followed, I found the logic tough to dance around. How much good had I really done as an activist, buzzing like a fly in the ear of corporate interests and government officials until I was swatted away? Had I done anything beyond delay the inevitable?

There was a ruthlessness about Adams, certainly. But maybe that's what the environmental movement needed: a little edge. Just look at what we were up against.

Adams had other qualities as well. An unabashed nature enthusiast, he spent several hours a week teaching me to scuba dive, pointing out stingrays and iridescent octopuses as we hovered in the bath-warm sea. He was also a leader who let lizards sprint across his hands. A man who, when I criticized my lack of formal scientific training, told me I was better than science: "You believe in things without proving them."

Harder to look past was the fact that Adams ran Camp Hope like basic training: an operation designed to break a person down, then build them back up. Everyone, students and faculty alike, rose before dawn for pushups and five-mile runs, endurance swims off the coast. Then there was breakfast. Lessons. More pushups for every missed homework assignment or unmade bed. Next were excursions to local communities to promote campaigns like SAVE THE SEA TURTLES, or FISH ARE FRIENDS. Every hour rattled so full with purpose that by the end of the day, when I collapsed into my bunk—exhausted, sunburnt, bug-bitten—there was little time to question anything before doing it again.

But what was there to question, really? Were a few pushups really so bad? After all, I liked Eleuthera. Camp Hope. I liked the way our wind turbine flexed in the wind and the solar panels gazed into the sky. I liked showering in rainwater that tasted dark and mossy from cisterns stored beneath the buildings. I liked the biodiesel vans and the communal meals of rice and beans, hydroponic salad, and sugar apples from the orchard. I liked our mealtime conversations: the liberal arts girls comparing permaculture to Russian literature, ex-Mormon Charlie rambling on Ursa Major, the biologists trilling about the deep-sea sharks they were hoping to catch off the coastal shelf with long-lined hooks.

"We find them," said the biologists, gripping their forks, "who knows what kind of funding we'll pull." They were a sun-bleached bunch, hair shaggy, eyes bright. "Who knows," they said, with the trembling faith of the already-convinced. "Who knows . . ."

I liked the compost piles and the collective dishwashing and explaining veganism to students like dogma. Adams defined my teaching role vaguely. "Just talk," he said. "Don't think about it." So I gave students the ideas I'd been kicking around for years. I spoke about interconnectedness. Diversity as resilience. The webbed limbs of a banyan tree, dolphin pods, ant colonies: they were my infrastructure, my demographics, my guides. "It's all tied together," I told them, "ecology in all dimensions. Past and present. Reality and imagination."

My old life, I realized, had been filled with so much negativity. Printing pamphlets that no one would read—protesting Monsanto, BP, or Exxon—it had been more of a penance, a kind of martyrdom, than an honest effort at change. But now:

I liked the way the students nodded.

I liked way the palm trees nodded in the breeze, as if they agreed too.

The Eleutherans tried to till the soil with plows gifted from Boston charities. They fought the sweat on their brows, fought back questions of worthwhileness.

IDLE HANDS ARE THE DEVIL'S WORKSHOP

Hoping for answers, they looked to the sun, blazing hot and bored. Their linen shirts, their petticoats, they wore them stained and tattered.

"Curry soil," the locals call it nowadays.
So full of rocks. Hard work. Dirty work.
A farmer feeds his cow two mangoes, eats the third himself.

Camp Hope's wind turbine broke first; the small rotor corroded.

"We'll hook back up to the grid," said Adams, knowing Camp Hope's solar panels couldn't handle the load alone. "But it's just temporary."

And it was temporary, except a week later we had nine days of rain—including a real tropical slasher that tore the roof off the bike shed and flooded both dormitories.

Adams, though, seemed almost pleased by the destruction. "Lock and load," he called to the students, as they carried sacks of rice from the storeroom to soak up excess water. Hefting a sack on each shoulder, he strode through the swill of flooded books and papers, splashing the sacks down before vaulting back for more.

That was the first time I really noticed Fitz Oberman—or noticed his behavior. While the other students followed Adams with soldierly enthusiasm, happy to be under his bark, Fitz stood beneath an arbor of passion fruit vines, sulking.

"Buck up," I said, slapping him on the back so that he stumbled forward a few paces. Camp Hope's daily exercise regime had made me stronger than I realized.

Fitz stared at me from under the brim of a large floppy hat. A pale kid, his blond curls almost albino, the hat was a necessity— one he doubtlessly resented—its goofiness at odds with what, under other circumstances, might have been a rather regal face.

"I want to make a phone call," he said. "I want to go home. I hate it here."

I said nothing. The righteous blaze in Fitz's eyes cooled to trepidation. By policy, Camp Hope restricted student communication back home. "For complete immersion and focus," according to Adams. Faculty sent frequent progress reports to parents, but within Camp Hope itself, homesickness was considered an affront to the community.

"I'd like—"

"I understood you the first time," I interrupted, checking that none of the other students had overheard. It would be bad for morale, that kind of talk, and "morale maintenance" was one area where Adams and I had a consistent ideological overlap.

The other students, though, were still cheerfully transporting sacks of rice. Adams lifted four sacks onto his shoulders at once, much to their fawning astonishment.

"How about we focus on helping out here?" I smiled at Fitz—I'd always been able to make friends with most people—but something about him had me on edge. I watched him lick his lips, draw in a breath. He seemed to be gathering strength for additional arguments, perhaps a more conspicuous tantrum, so I added, "I'll call your parents right away and discuss the matter."

The lie slipped out so easily, I barely noticed.

Telephone poles march down the coast, the orange caress of love-vines winding between wires. Even from the windows of a moving van, I can see the giant roadside spider webs; their fist-sized makers braced against the breeze.

I pull into a settlement. Locals sit on stoops in twos and threes. One woman sells frozen tamarind juice in plastic cups—sweet brown popsicles. Chickens flutter past ankles. "Call me Rosenie," she says, without a smile.

There are no jobs. The people leak away, like freshwater through the ground: Lutra's limestone like a sieve. The kids all go to Nassau. They go to Miami. On Sundays, people gather in sweaty churches to praise God and pray the resorts will return.

But still there is food in the sea. At least there is food in the sea.

Our students hand out flyers. THE IMPACTS OF OVERFISHING. *I ask her not to eat the grouper, the conch, to leave the mangrove swamps unsprayed.*

KEEP THIS PLACE PRISTINE; KEEP IT BEAUTIFUL.

Rosenie looks at me, fanning her face with a straw hat. She leans against her cooler of tamarind cups. She pours her eyes all over me; she pours, what I assume, is merely curiosity.

Only later do I realize it was fury.

The heavy rains did not return, but in their wake the sand fly population exploded. Everyone's legs and arms became spotted with bites, itchy red welts like chicken pox that lasted days at a time. Most students handled the bites well; they made an effort not to scratch; they made a game of it. But Fitz—I pulled him aside one day after class, having noticed his welts were clawed at and oozy.

"Scratching just makes it worse," I said, as the classroom emptied to only us.

Fitz reached down and began scratching in front of me.

I drew in a breath, knowing I needed to approach Fitz with "positive alternatives," as Adams had suggested in our most recent faculty meeting. "Take him spear fishing, crab hunting, free diving," he'd said. "Let him know he matters." In the growing humidity, Adams had taken to conducting the meetings shirtless so that while the rest of us sweated and swatted flies, he looked like Rambo, at ease in a desk chair, a shark tooth necklace slung around his throat.

"But why can't we just let him go home?" one of the liberal arts girls had asked. Marjorie, an oversunscreened thing. She'd also had an unfortunate run-in with poisonwood earlier that week, the rashy results of which she still stoically endured.

"Let him go home?" Adams frowned. "We give every person a hundred and ten percent."

In my old life—my New York life—I might have quipped, "why not a hundred-twenty-five percent?" But Adams's methods were making more sense every day. I'd seen real progress with many of our students: kids whose dads owned banks were talking about getting solar panels for their schools, wind farms in their communities. And while everyone at Camp Hope had played a role in these transformations, I knew that many changes were my doing—my teaching—and I wanted Adams to recognize that fact: to see that I was the change-maker he'd brought me onboard to be.

"I'll work with Fitz," I said, sounding more enthusiastic than I felt. "He came to me first, so I'll see about getting him in leadership roles, getting him more engaged."

Adams nodded, pleased to have the issue resolved. There were other things to discuss, like the rumors of a new cruise ship development on the island.

Still, I sensed Adams studying me, reevaluating me, even as he said, "Great, let's talk fund-raising."

Actually dealing with Fitz, however, was another matter. Standing in the empty classroom, the kid continued scratching, fingers digging into his flesh in long slow pulls.

"Cut it out."

Fitz paused and straightened up. A smile wormed onto his lips. "You know," he said, as if our conversation were entirely casual, "the locals spray these things."

Of course I knew. I'd taught a lesson on pesticides: by killing insects with chemicals, we killed the birds that ate them, thereby poisoning the food chain. Ourselves.

Fitz returned to scratching, this time with a thoughtful rhythm.

I felt an itchiness rising in my own spotted limbs, then an urge to lash out, to scream into his smirking face.

Instead I took a breath, said, "You're late for trigonometry."

With that, I left the classroom and made a point of forgetting him.

I had plans to go scuba diving.

The morning curled open, beaming and dewy.

In another century, on the same sun-soaked island, the Eleutherans wondered if they'd been abandoned by their God. They needed more than a few spades and pewter spoons, the well wishes of Massachusetts Bay. Their corn crop failed, then the pumpkins and the peas. What seeds weren't devoured by rats, by land crabs, withered with a drought. To stave off hunger, the Eleutherans speared sea turtles and stubby-legged iguana. When insects become unbearable—chigoe fleas, sand flies, mosquitoes big as birds—they burned Caribbean pine, filled their homes with black smoke, for a few moments of reprieve. They looked at one another with red and weepy eyes. They searched their minds for proverbs but came up empty-handed.

They disbanded, rebanded, died.

At last, the few survivors held lanterns near reefs at night so that Spanish galleons, merchant ships, wrecked just off the coast. Then the Eleutherans salvaged barrels of ambergris, rum: the provisions of dead men that floated onto shore.

The day I found Fitz lying on the beach getting purposely burned, Adams got a call confirming the rumors of a cruise ship port slated for construction.

"Don't even start," I muttered, marching Fitz to the first aid station. What with the chaos of the morning—Adams bellowing at Bahamian officials over the phone, then rushing to catch a flight to Nassau—I had been craving some downtime.

But here was Fitz, slumped on a medical bunk: his skin seared red, his chapped lips groaning, "Just let me go home."

Rather than answering, I looked out the first aid station window. A few feathery clouds lolled over a cerulean sea. I thought about what Adams had asked me before leaving. "Can I count on you, Dawn?" he'd said. "Can you keep this place in line?"

I could, I realized: my competence staring back like a woman I'd only just met.

"I'm not the only one." Fitz pushed himself up onto his elbows. "Others want to leave too."

Annoyed, I returned to his bedside, gripping his shoulder to inspect the sunburn. He sank down, wincing from the pressure. "You really expect me to believe you?" I tried to sound unfazed— to feel unfazed—and yet it had never occurred to me that more students might harbor the same sentiments as Fitz. They all seemed so diligent, so enthusiastic.

Or, perhaps, so well trained.

"It's true, they—"

I slapped some salve onto Fitz's bare skin.

He cried out once, his eyes looking somewhere I couldn't see.

How far away did the Eleutherans feel, watching the first ship splinter on a reef, the boat's wooden belly lacerated, drowning sailors crying out? Did England feel distant, then? Did the Eleutherans feel far away as they stood knee-deep in the sea, a salted breeze muffling the acrid burn of lantern resin?

Or was the Old World suddenly close?

At dinner, the students asked when Adams would be back.

"Soon," I told them.

"But when?" repeated a pony-tailed girl; the other students looked distraught.

I ignored them and scanned the dining hall, hands on my hips, projecting the fiercely competent woman I'd discovered I could be. No more wispy Brooklyn burnout. Two months of sun and exercise had turned my skin leathery, my muscles hard.

In a corner of the dining hall, I caught sight of Fitz talking to several wide-eyed boys. While I would have been pleased, a week ago, to see him making friends, now I worried he was trying to stage some kind of coup.

"Table seven," I called, as Fitz's jaw froze midsentence. "Fifteen pushups."

"But, we—"

"Fifteen. Or I'll raise it."

Without further protest, the boys dropped to the floor—even Fitz—their skinny elbows bending to ninety degrees. The other students, having noted my tone, began filing toward dishwashing duty or compost brigade.

Meanwhile, the biologists huddled together, chattering about their long-lined hooks. Recently, just off the coastal shelf—a two-thousand-foot drop not far from shore—they'd hauled up the head of a tiger shark, its toothy jaw impaled on their bait. Just the head, though. The rest of the shark was chewed off.

"It's down there," I heard a biologist say, meaning an even bigger shark, more ancient. More impossible.

The liberal arts girls talked about eating ice cream.

As soon as I could get away, I went diving.

One hundred feet down, your mind gets scrambled. Nitrogen narcosis it's called: a giddiness, a phantasmagoria. To Cousteau: "the rapture of the deep." That far down, it's harder to draw air from a regulator. Harder to see. Colors go dim, red especially.

"Ain't good to be alone," Nehemiah had told me. "A man shouldn't be by his lone self. Or a fee-male, in your case."

Alone, underwater, I run my flashlight over the swaying inflections of fan coral, the glint of eyes secreted in rocks. Sea grass quivers like souls before God. I see the open mouth of a crevasse—an underwater cave—and slip inside, careful not to let my fins touch the polyps lining the walls. The crevasse turns into a tunnel that falls away into darkness. I hover above the coastal shelf, an aquanaut, weightless in three dimensions.

My mask begins to fog. I have an urge to tear it off, as if that might help me see, perhaps even to glimpse the deep-sea sharks the biologists believe are swimming below. I stare into the chasm, remind myself to breathe.

Only air bubbles know where to go. They stream past me toward the surface.

In a world even older than the Eleutherans', the Lucayan people told stories to explain themselves. Their ancestors lived in caves, they said, but only caves. They could not leave, because the sun would turn them into a rock or a tree. But one day a hero tricked the sun. The hero convinced the sun to stare at its own reflection: the image cast into the sea. The sun looked and was blinded. The people were set free.

Then, *La Niña. La Pinta. La Santa Maria.* Spanish galleons threading their way through the archipelago, black-prowed needles sewing up fate. Columbus must have known not to look at his reflection: the proud nose cast in Bahamian waters.

The Eleutherans saw theirs, but years too late.

With Adams away, everyone was restless. The liberal arts girls, abandoning their usual shyness, appeared in my bedroom, twittering and effervescent. They wanted to go dancing.

"Please, Dawn," they said. "Please, please, please."

Down island, there was a village with a bar. Rum and ginger beer. Lukewarm cans of Kalik.

"It'll be fun. We won't be gone long . . ."

Adams expected the faculty to spend their nights at Camp Hope—and, tired as we usually were, we had no reason to argue—but that evening the island beckoned, its winding footpaths perfumed with frangipani, veiled in purple shadows.

And anyways, Adams didn't have to know.

At the bar, Caribbean melodies trickled from a three-man band, one guy strumming a rusty saw. Some locals seemed amused by our presence, while others became tight-lipped and wary. Bat moths fluttered to the ceiling. Photos of celebrities lined the barroom walls. A bat moth landed on Madonna's face, like a big black moustache.

I got drunk easily. Maybe because it had been so long, or maybe because of the heat: the small room warmed by so many bodies, by heavy breaths and sidelong glances. Soon enough my T-shirt was soaked with sweat, even though I barely danced, just stood swaying in a corner.

Outside a moon ripened.

I felt out-of-body. Displaced. I began wondering what had happened to that warmhearted woman from Brooklyn: the one who loved to love. When was the last time I'd even thought about sex? When had sex become just another word for compromise?

The liberal arts girls, having tugged one another in front of the band, were swooped up in the arms of local men. The skinny one, Angela, looked around for someone to laugh to: she was dancing with the fisherman. His chapped hands slipped into the curve of her back, his mouth moving to her neck. "You turn me on, baby," he said, his lips spelling out every word. She ignored this, kept her smile locked. She made him twirl her in the dress she had gotten from Macy's.

Meanwhile, old folks studied us, our awkward dancing, from benches set along the room's edge. We couldn't move the way their daughters could.

"Those island women"—Charlie, the ex-Mormon, bumped against me, out of breath and whispering like a co-conspirator— "they got a lot of—"

I clutched my drink, trying to remember what I'd come here to do.

But already it was ending. The locals piled into old cars, into truck beds, and rumbled away into the night. I walked the two miles to Camp Hope, the liberal arts girls trailing behind, sandals held in their hands. Once back, I fell asleep quickly, drunk enough not to notice the sand flies. The stale air. My own starving heart.

In the morning, I would tell these people to leave the conch in the sea, to leave their crops unsprayed. I would tell them it was for their own good. For everyone's good. I would tell them to forget the possibility of a cruise ship port. To forget the jobs they pray for like long-lost apostles. To forget, forget, forget.

I eat a passion fruit growing wild on a vine, its insides a cluster of wrinkly yellow green. Seeds like fish eggs slither down my throat. Does passion always taste this sour? Cape Hope's classrooms are starting to smell like the schools I try not to remember: stale coffee, urine, mildewing books.

Test question #1: When did the first slave ships arrive?

Stray dogs wander in and out through doors left open for the breeze. Some of the dogs have dingo in them, people say, mixed in when the boats came from Africa.

Test question #2: When did the last slave ships leave?

It must mean something that Spanish vessels ferried bodies

*away from the island to work and die on foreign soil. And not
so long after, other boats brought bodies back. The Eleutherans'
descendants: British loyalists. Plantation owners with new ideas
of paradise.*

Test question #3: And what is it—your idea of paradise—what
is it exactly?

(a) The red petals of hibiscus flowers pressed closed like the
folds of a lady's skirt.

(b) A quivering Casuarina pine, shaking free a thousand
needles.

(c) Those many-footed mangroves, stooped and wading
through their salty parlors.

Or maybe:

(d) None of the above.

It was still dark when I rattled the bunks of several students. They
snapped to attention, shaking off drowsiness to ask, "Did we miss
roll call? Are we in trouble?"

I told them no, but to get moving. To gather their notebooks and
cameras. "We're going on a field trip," I announced, in spite of my
head-clawing hangover. "I want you to see the site of the proposed
cruise ship port—a pristine cove—I'll be expecting an essay."

Really, though, the trip wasn't for them. I'd woken needing to
see what Adams called "unspeakably important": the beach that
would otherwise be encrusted with tiki huts and rubber slides. I
needed to remind myself what we were working to save.

Our van chugged down island, trailing French-fry fumes. Fitz
sulked in the back, but the other students babbled, bright-eyed
and excited, which took the edge off my headache.

A MAN DIGS HIS GRAVE WITH HIS OWN TEETH, the Eleutherans once
said, even with mouths full of gravel, tongues coated in sand—AS
YOU SOW SO YOU SHALL REAP.

"Pole bean, mel'n, goat peppa."
  The air stings with ash from slash and burn.
"Cabbage, tomata, cassava."

But you can't eat ethics, can you?
"Locusts, they chewed all them haloon"
Can you?

I pulled the van onto a sandy side road, spilled out with the students. Broken glass crunched underfoot. In the distance: the weathered cement shells of several buildings, water winking through the crooked legs of a stilted lifeguard chair.

"I thought we were going to a pristine beach?" said a student.

I checked my map again, just as bewildered.

This was definitely the place.

Further on, the ground turned tiled, cracked stairs leading to a swimming pool filled with brackish water. A drowned golf cart.

"C-l-u—," said a boy, peeling back a curtain of vines to read a tiled wall. "Club Med."

I knew I should say something about the resilience of nature, but I felt suddenly tired. My hangover crept back. I wanted to curl up in the ruins and sleep a hundred years.

"Where's Fitz?" said another student.

There'd be no sleeping: of course Fitz would wander off. I cursed, perhaps too loudly, then told the students to follow as I began jogging around the old resort calling his name.

Half an hour of hunting and still no sign of him.

We regrouped. The students stood circled around me, hands at their sides, dutifully awaiting my next instruction. And yet I couldn't help thinking how outnumbered I was.

"You would tell me if you knew where he was?" I said, giving them each a hard stare in turn. "You would tell me, right?"

The students stared back, sweaty and confused. One girl looked about to cry.

"Drink some water," I said, regretting my accusations, but noticing, also, the dwindling daylight. "Hydrate," I told the students, "then we'll do another sweep."

This time we extended the search, circling out to the beach, even peering up the legs of the lifeguard chair. We whistled; we shouted until our throats grew hoarse.

Still nothing.

The students—unflappable—continued sifting the landscape,

but I paused and began trying to formulate an explanation. Fitz got lost? Ran away? Evaporated?

In the late afternoon sun, the sea sat silvery and oblivious. I almost felt jealous. That horizon line, so effortlessly smooth, like a single sheet of polished metal.

Except for something—a floating something—about thirty yards out.

The pale limbs of a body.

"Ms. Vargus!"

A student was running toward me, wild with news. I braced myself for the onset of guilt, the heart-squeeze of failed responsibility.

Then I discovered I was fine.

"Fitz—" the girl, breathless, nearly barreled into me, her fingers pointing—though not at the sea, as I'd expected—pointing down the beach at a set of tracks.

I looked at the body again: a hunk of driftwood.

They were freed, the Lucayans told one another, when the sun saw his reflection.

The Puritans named the island "Eleuthera," a Greek word for freedom.

"Freeman status?" the plantation owners asked. "How about apprenticeship?"

Club Med: "Be free and fabulous."

I found Fitz in a cave like a yawning mouth.

"What the hell do you think you're doing?" My question ricocheted off the high ceiling, the damp limestone walls.

Fitz didn't answer. Instead he sat cross-legged, serene. His gaze flickered to an oblong boulder near the front of the cave: a rock oddly shaped like a lectern—a pulpit.

"Make a speech," he said. His pale face leered, spectral in the half-light.

By then the other students had drifted into the cave as well. They wandered about, heads tipped back to stare at the high ceiling, as if looking for the origins of echoes. Whatever Fitz was getting at, I decided to ignore. "Okay, show's over," I said. "Everyone back to the van."

"Make a speech," Fitz repeated, this time louder.

The other students stilled, went quiet.

"You're not feeling well, Fitz." I tried to sound calm, even bored. "You have sunstroke—that's why you got lost—we need to get you back to school."

He didn't move. I glanced at the rock again, its unusual shape. Was there something magnetic about it? I imagined my hands on the rock's surface: smooth and cool.

"Come on, Ms. Vargas." Fitz's words echoed and expanded, as if channeling a thousand voices, a chorus of the dead. "Tell us about paradise, about a better world."

The other students stared at me, waiting.

The Harvard Students stare at me, waiting.

If I could, I would say this: after Columbus pushed his way to the boat's bow for the first view of land; after the last Lucayan died huddled in a cave and the Eleutherans starved, then baited ships; after the plantation fields—rows of cotton, spires of pineapple stalks, the whip crack of progress—after the rum-runners, the Navy base, the resorts that burned coppice for golf course grass, named themselves "Cotton Bay," "Pineapple Point"; after the hurricane; after tarmacs became landing sites for drug planes instead of princesses and tennis stars; after settlements emptied to only slaves' ancestors and Haitian refugees and a few sunburnt whites sequestered up in Gregorytown, all of them—black or white—drunk on nostalgia; when all that was left of the Lucayans was a few chipped bits of palmetto ware, there was us.

"Don't you believe?" said Fitz. "Aren't you a believer?"

He began laughing—or choking—his head lolling back, the noise crowding the cave like the beating wings of bats.

"Sunstroke," I told the other students, as I wrenched Fitz to his feet and hustled him back to the van. "Sunstroke," I told myself.

In the dark of night, water pours from the sky, slips through limestone like a sieve.

A joke no one seems to get.

Nehemiah holds out his hands and looks toward heaven. Water leaks through his fingers. The drop drop drop of tears.

We returned to Camp Hope later than planned, but no one seemed to have noticed. Everyone was busy celebrating the work of the biologists. Earlier that day, they'd pulled a monstrous primeval shark from the depths. Eyes an iridescent green, six radiator gills. The shark had never seen light the way we had, swimming so deep: the length of the Empire State Building beneath our boats.

"Halleluiah," Adams boomed on the phone, when I described the discovery. "We're going to have research vessels up and down the coast! They'll never get that cruise ship port with this in our back pockets. This is damn fine news. Damn fine. And on that note, Dawn, you ready to become assistant director?"

Under the surface of the sea, the surface of memory—that taut lip of time—they swim back and forth, as they've done for millennia. Those ancient things we barely believe exist: pulled from the water like drowned secrets. A species that outlasted the dinosaurs. They circle us still, eyes filtering an eternal twilight. They had seen it all, every item that sank to the ocean floor: every spear or hymnal, doubloon, manacle, pearl necklace. Every pen and student notebook.

"The Lucayan people had a myth," I tell the Harvard students, at last beginning my speech. "Once, their people lived in a cave, unable to leave, for fear the sun would turn them to stone."

And they listen, as they always listen.

Free Love

By the time I was fifteen, I had fallen in love eight times, and things showed no sign of slowing down. "Leave the tall boys for the tall girls," my grandnana says, but she knows I get attached to all kinds of people. Thick, thin, black, white, strong, feeble, obstreperous, prosperous, peckish, mustached, freckled, unibrowed, eye-patched.

"Love is grand," Nana says. "Divorce is a hundred grand."

But my parents taught me that love is like having to pee really bad. Or like expatriation from Zimbabwe when one is suspected of espionage and possibly treason.

Sometimes it can't be helped.

Sunday rolls in without asking anyone's permission. I'm languishing in my bedroom, drenched in the usual listlessness of a stranded inamorata. Nana's in the kitchen, odds-on that she's got one hand in a mixing bowl, one eye toward my bedroom door. I can hear her rattling through cupboards, spitting out aphorisms like a wrinkled old almanac. "Some people are like blisters," she says. "They only appear when the work is done." This is followed by a volley of throat clearing and expectant spoon tapping.

Nana speaks in the language of old wives—wives who've slipped themselves a little something, if you know what I mean—so she gets that I like sayings I can bite, chew, and put in my pocket for later. And, if there wasn't an envelope stuffed with Uncomfortable Content leering at me from my bedroom dresser, I might act less like a blister and more like the sort of person Nana prefers: namely, someone who leaves her bedroom to help make carrot coleslaw and freeze homemade orange juice popsicles.

Earlier today, when Dr. Virginia "Call-Me-Gina" Eubanks, PhD, put down her notepad, smoothed her blouse, and remarked, "Ms. Joy, I know you are unusual—I mean I know your situation is unusual," I assumed she was referencing my particular knowledge and concern for the neoliberal indigenous movement mobilizing in Ecuador. Then again, she may have noticed my fondness for twig tea and pickled-beet salad. There's even a chance she was alluding to my mother, who took an acid trip three months ago and hasn't come back, or to my father, whose alarmingly progressive leadership of the Free Oaks Commune caught the attention of the federal government, or to my own grimly disorienting reality as an uprooted flower child sent to live with a woman who owns four types of muffin pans and tablecloths for every holiday.

But I couldn't tell from the tone of her voice.

Sixty-four days ago, I was plucked from Free Oaks by two aunts and one lawyer, all buzzing with compassion and heroism.

"She can't live in that madhouse," said my aunts. "Feds are gonna shut the whole place down any minute. It's a regular doped-up circus freak show."

"Precisely," said the lawyer. "It's niiiiiineteen-eighty-three. No one has patience for this hippie business anymore."

Now I've grown up thinking I was a revolution and a half; that's why I went along with the whole thing. Father always told us that existential alignment requires living inside-out and upside-down, and I was hard-pressed to come up with anything more inside-out than moving from Free Oaks back onto the grid.

"It's for the best," my aunts promised, as I sat pinned between them in a station wagon trundling across the country. "We just want you to have a stable home life, a little structure, some family support."

They dropped me off at Nana's.

It was early August then, and as I stood blinking in the dusty wake of my aunts' station wagon, I felt fear swirling up in my stomach like a bad lunch. Nana stood beside me, gripping my rucksack. She was certainly on the sturdy side, with thick eyebrows, a tumbling pile of gray hair, and sleeves rolled up past her elbows. "Help family members in need and they'll always remember you," she said, watching my aunts drive away, "the next time they are in need."

To be honest I wasn't sure if she was talking to me or to herself. That was the first time I'd met Nana. My mother had never offered much in the way of ancestral characterization, except to say that her parents were real style-cramping squares. This was more or less confirmed when Nana turned to me, sniffed the air, and said I better make a beeline for the shower. Not being one to abandon my principles, I told her that I would not be showering. Everyone at Free Oaks felt best when scented by pine needles and damp earth.

Nana raised one large eyebrow.

I didn't want to start off with sore feelings, so I told her I would go swimming later that afternoon.

"You know," said Nana, as she offered quick salute to the neighbors lurking nearby with watering cans and leashed little terriers. "You're gonna have to make some changes. We don't run loose around here. We wash our hands before dinner."

"You and who?" I asked, looking down at the fingernails I kept dirty on principle.

"Us," she said, wrapping me snugly in her rules and leading me inside.

People love me. They drag their chairs across the school cafeteria for a better view. I am ten steps west of anything my new friends think they understand, and all the more fascinating because of it.

"Your name is Almond Joy?" they say, their faces incredulous, bamboozled, starstruck. "Like the candy bar?"

"Exactly like," I reply. "It's Positive Occupation of Corporate Lingual Hegemony."

"That is Unbelievable. Phenomenal. Magnificent. But—"

"But what?"

"What is someone like you doing in place like Winfield?"

"Someone like me?" I can be a legendary tease.

"We thought you moved here from some sort of hippie commune." *Hippie* is pronounced delicately, as if the word is anatomical or unstable.

"I suppose you could call it that," I say.

"So you grew your own food?"

"Yes."

"And you shared everything?"

"Yes."

"And you lived in a yurt and walked around barefoot and never went to real school, but instead learned from an extended family of bohemians and artists and sexologists and burnt-out Berkeley professors, and it was all about harmony and life-flow, about non-dualistic empathic communion and synergistic attunement, and no one took showers or told you when to go to bed, and everyone felt that the earth was one great ship and you were all sailing through a beautiful and mysterious universe?"

"Yes, more or less like that," I reply brightly. "That and child neglect, material poverty, and television deprivation."

"It just seems rather atypical," said Gina, PhD, as we sat in her office, "that someone with test scores as high as yours would have such a difficult time getting settled."

"I know!" I said, as if I too were surprised by this fact.

She leaned forward, and I leaned in as well, recognizing that at this very moment, Gina was about to share her greatest secret.

"You have to understand," she explained. "It is important to be yourself, but not too much yourself."

I nodded, even though this psychologist's greatest secret was nothing to boast about. At Free Oaks, I had perched in the laps of transient poets and tugged at the robes of bilingual *maharishi,* collecting nuggets of enlightenment like stones. My head had been stuffed full with meanings-of-life for as long as I could remember.

Gina wasn't done, though. "Think of it this way," she said, sitting back in her chair and crossing one leg over the other. "Daisies grow in Winfield, but orchids don't."

She smiled, pleased with her metaphor. I smiled too, leaning back in my own chair and crossing one leg over the other. I had noticed there were a lot of daisies.

"Do you have any hobbies, Almond?" she continued, her voice as smooth as soap.

Nana rustles outside my door.

"You gonna have something for me to mail tomorrow?" she says.

I tell her my letter is in the works, then listen for the fading shuffle of feet. She stays put. The woman could smell a fib from a mountaintop. I glance at the envelope—untouched—and consider inviting her inside.

But Nana isn't finished. "There's someone on the phone for you," she says, as if this happens all the time.

I shoot out of my room, skid down the hallway, and lunge for the telephone, pressing the receiver to my ear.

"Almond?" says a voice, and for a moment I think it's my father. "Almond Joy? This is Clark Butler. We have home economics together on Thursdays."

Clark is the kind of boy who flosses his teeth every day, who writes prompt thank-you notes and reads books by Charles Dickens because he believes they will be good for him.

"I hope you are well," he says, with the voice of a budding professional. "I'm calling to ask if you might like to go out sometime. Maybe this Friday, six o'clock?"

I'm already swooning over his interest in timetables and protocol. He's the most inside-out prospect to come along yet.

"Almond? Are you still on the line?"

I envision our date: *The two of us wedged in a vinyl diner booth. He orders a chocolate milkshake, and I ask for a straw-berry-vanilla-coffee combination, which he finds attractively bold. He says that his father is an investment banker, that they go fishing together every summer and his mother packs them each a bacon ham sandwich (his favorite), that the two of them are planning on selling their boat to buy a bigger one. He tells me that he loves Civil War history, roots for the Dodgers and that his parents' twentieth anniversary is next week. They go out to eat every year. Sometimes they come home from the restaurant as late as eleven o'clock.*

I slouch in my seat, sipping my milkshake, drugged by his description of a two-parent, housebound breeding. When his words run dry, I suck my straw loudly, and say something that goes down easy—like, I think I may have lived in Constanti-nople in a past life. Or, have you ever wondered about the shape of the universe? Maybe it's really a giant hand and we're all just roaming fingers!

He looks at me, his eyes wide.

And I keep talking, describing the contours of acorn shells, the many uses for goldenseal and amaranth. My voice sounds like music. He forgets what it's like to be afraid.

You can help me open my mind, he says.

Open your mind too much and your brain falls out, I reply, even though the words are Nana's and not my own. I'll feel sick. I'll have finished my milkshake too fast.

Standing in the kitchen, I tug the phone cord around my body in an elastic embrace. It's been over two months since I moved to Winfield, but every day after school, I flutter around the house like a trapped bat, which Nana says gives her the willies.

"Almond?" Clark's voice squeaks slightly. "You still there?"

Outside the house I'll be loose; I'll be lost. There's so much love sloshing around inside me and no way to keep it all in. No way to plug up old leaks.

"Next Friday?" I say, trying to sound weary, like the women I've started watching on TV. "Oh geez, sorry Clark, I've got plans then."

I bury the receiver and uncoil the cord. Then I wish he'd call back so that I could pretend I'd been kidding.

He doesn't. I scoot to the living room and give Nana's knitting needles a go. I've got some experience in free-form macramé, and she's got enough yarn to make an iceberg cozy.

As it turns out, though, I've only got enough patience in me to keep an ice cube warm.

"Jeanette never got the hang of a purl stitch either." Nana has arrived in the living room with a feather duster and an eye toward the photo frames spread along the mantel. My mother, I'm reminded, had another name before Buttercup. Nana picks up a photo and I put down my needles. We look at the portrait of a girl wearing a pink headband and pearl earrings, gazing at the camera with thoughtful eyes.

"Never run after a bus or a man," Nana says. "There'll always be another."

Other faces line the mantel as well. A soldier, beardless and solemn, in a black-buttoned jacket. A husband and wife, frozen side by side.

"That Clark fellow seemed nice on the phone," Nana suddenly seems to remember.

"He was on the dull side," I tell her. "All establishment and no bag."

Nana resumes dusting the photo of a daughter she hasn't seen since '67. For such an efficient woman, she wipes the frame slowly. I can tell we are both wondering the same thing: wondering whether my mother would still be wearing cardigans if she hadn't met my father, whether she would have been the kind of woman who went to PTA meetings and made grocery lists and remembered birthdays, whether she would have allowed her daughter to wander freely in the muddy cacophony of a music festival with the only stipulation being that she catch the van by morning.

We wonder if meeting my father made her more happy or less happy.

There's more yarn under the coffee table, Nana tells me. I should pull some out if I want to keep-on-keeping-on with my knitting. She's got more dusting to do.

I was made in a psychedelic rainstorm, in an eruption of cosmic synergy, in the warm updraft of the Summer of Love.

At least, that's how my mother explained it to me when I was six.

"It was in a field," she said, exhaling a plume of cinnamony smoke that billowed into every crevasse and eddy of our yurt. My mother patted my head, absentmindedly handing me her lighter to play with. "A field of dandelions."

"Baby, you are all mixed up." My father was sprawled beside her, braiding a tendril of his hair. "It was the night after the rally. In the Blue Room. Remember?"

"Or was it the beach?" They grabbed one another's hands. "Beneath the harvest moon—"

They kept talking and remembering and not remembering and putting their hands on one another's faces.

I wandered off through the commune. A little girl in a dirty dress, looking for someone to take me in their lap, or to play guitar—but mostly for the Berkeley professors, who might give me something their minds were tired of holding.

Gina wasn't the kind of therapist who liked to roll with the unresolved. "Almond, would you mind telling me more about your father?" she said, as if Freud had snuck into the office and whispered something in her ear. I recited the standard profile. Raised Catholic. Left home at eighteen. Traveled through India. Became successively infatuated by the teachings of the Hare Krishna, the *Bhagavad Gita*, and B. F. Skinner. Convinced he could revolutionize society by starting his own. Staked claim to an abandoned farm in California with eight initial followers, including my mother. A brilliant orator. Lanky, blond, roguishly unshaven. Remarkably charismatic.

"Okay," she said, "but what about *your* relationship with him, specifically?"

I wanted to like Gina. She complimented my earrings when we first met and seemed to know what she was doing. But she was all about accuracy and operandi and sharpened pencils. She'd never lived like I had: never woken up in the warm vacuum of a day without edges, never slept in the quivering space of an unfulfilled promise.

Let love fill you up, my father used to say with amused exasperation when I shook him out of his meditation to ask if anyone was fixing a meal. *Learn to give away everything and want nothing in return. That's the greatest gift of all.*

I would look down at my empty belly, put my hands in empty pockets.

And he would keep talking, addressing the other revolutionaries as they gathered around, intrigued and impressed by the out-loud ideals of a courageous new counterculture.

Be a sponge. Soak up stories, he'd say. Look at the family we have here. Look at all the fathers and mothers and brothers and sisters we have. Be fulfilled by each other, by the energy, the vibrations—

"You want to know about my father?" I said to Gina, taking each syllable like a steep step. "He loved a lot of people."

She nodded, urging me on. "And what about you?"

"What about me?" I echoed.

Gina wanted to hear about the bodies that slipped in and out of Free Oaks, hovering in my embrace before pressing on. She wanted me to tell her about the kisses misplaced in the slow chaos of an unregulated life. About the boys. About the men.

But even in the space of my own memories, I felt forgotten.

"Well, Gina," I finally declared, "to me, love is having nothing and wanting nothing. That's the greatest gift of all."

"When you gonna mail that letter, Almond?" Nana says, plunging her hands into the kitchen sink suds to do dishes.

"It's getting done," I tell her.

She pins down a baking pan, scrubbing hard, as if the thing might bite back.

I'm still trying to feel out the rhythms of a place with cupboards and coasters. I finger Nana's Highly Breakable Fine China. The teacups and the plates stand at attention, as if testifying on behalf of an antique marriage.

"Do you miss Gramps?" I ask.

She says she's gotten used to missing him and knocks off a catalogue of aphorisms about moving on, things changing, and making the best of a tough situation. I realize she's got an inventory for a reason. As she speaks, she looks stronger, as if losing someone you care about doesn't have to mean losing yourself as well.

I tell her I've been considering falling in love again.

She tells me the dishes aren't drying themselves.

When I last saw my mother, she'd kicked back a whole lot of something—we weren't sure what—and had been tripping for three days straight.

No one paid much attention, though. My father had two fresh flower children to liberate from uptight understandings of sexual relations, and everyone else was wigged-out over the Feds' threats to crash Free Oaks.

"I've gotta split for a while," I told my mother, who lay in a dark corner of our yurt, swaddled in blankets. "Least until all this blows over. I'm getting put up with some relatives."

She did not respond, only clenched and unclenched her pendants and her beads, peering into me like I was a window.

"Mum, do you hear—"

She grabbed my wrist, pulling me close. "It's better to be a circle than a square," she said, half whispering, half singing in my ear. "Don't you know? Are you listening?"

She burped and started giggling, her laughter turning into gasps that became sobs. "I—than—can't—"

I held her hand and told her that she was my oracle, that I was listening. I was always trying so hard to listen.

She moaned, spit dribbling down her chin.

Outside the yurt, my aunts honked from their station wagon. I tucked my mother under another quilt and grabbed my rucksack, walking toward the car as slow as I could in case she called me back. In case anyone called me back. All I heard, though, was the irked strain of a sitar and the faint warble of displaced giggles somewhere across the commune.

Gina ended our session by saying some things about attending school regularly, wearing a bra, and scheduling our next session.

I wanted to show her that I was really trying, that I was more than the damaged result of an adult preoccupation with self-indulgence, so I paused in the doorway to her office before leaving. "In the future," I said, standing up straight and annunciating my vowels, "I hope to be a lawyer, or possibly a news anchor."

I wasn't sure if this was my real hope, but I liked the taste of these ideas on my tongue. I wondered what a pantsuit would feel like: if it would wear like armor or a disguise. If it would feel like treason.

At any rate, Gina seemed to find my announcement compelling. She told me I was making some real progress. She was looking forward to seeing me again.

In my bedroom, I read my name written across the envelope sent by my father. His letter is scratched in the margins of a folded flyer for Pascal's Lagoon Monkeys, in the small sharp letters of a man who would colonize the moon if you gave him time.

Almond,
Remember the Family's collective freedom-visualization?
It was a ship with no anchor. We have realized that dream.
We are all in a houseboat off the coast of Mexico. The Man's
intrusion onto the farm may have been for the better.
We Have Never Been This Free. Don't let them close your
mind. Return to us! Your Mother has been mentioning you.
Love,
Dad

It takes twelve sheets of paper and three broken pencils to respond, but in the end, all I manage to write is, *I can't,* even though I can, and even though I miss it all terribly.

My father will know I am lying. They all will. I could rejoin the Free Oaks Family and live in a houseboat and sail around the world. The idea sounds spectacularly imprecise, gloriously undeveloped. My only hope is that he understands I'm trying, in my own way, to live inside-out and upside-down. All I can do is seal the letter before my mind changes.

I'm all wound up again. I read the beginning of five novels I've been saving, making myself quit after the first page, though each book begs me to continue. I think about Clark and about my father and about all the times I'll have to say no, and I decide that this is penance.

Then I decide it's practice.

When I was ten, we had a bonfire. It was fifteen feet tall and glowed in the night like a hot head of hair.

"You can study how combustion precipitates thermal equilibrium as a result of its inherent differential symmetry," the professors told me, before collapsing into giggles.

Salvador toasted crackers on a flat rock, Jack coaxed drumbeats from an upside-down bowl, Clover sang a song about morning glories, and everyone stood a little too close to the fire. We jumped back when its flames lashed toward us. We let the ash sink into our hair and settle on our pores.

Then some of Sal's crackers slipped into the fire, charring instantly. My father just laughed and tossed in an apple he'd been chewing. Soon, everyone was whooping, emptying their hands and pockets. Letters, dollars, bracelets, pills, pictures, all leapt into the flames like the willing victims of a sacrifice. Jack beat harder on his drums, keeping pace until someone threw them in too.

"Get the books," someone said.

"Burn the past," said another.

"A fresh start, man! A new day."

I watched as anthologies, encyclopedias, poems—the guts of our tiny commune library—fluttered and dove into the fire.

"I wrote that one," said a professor, as his book sizzled and burned.

Clover and Sal were dancing.

"Isn't it marvelous, Almond? It's all happening!" exclaimed my mother, tearing off her clothes to add them as well.

"Don't look so nervous, little lady," my father teased. "We won't throw you in too."

I am sixteen now, and I've been heartbroken enough to know love isn't easy. Thick, thin, black, white, strong, feeble, obstreperous, prosperous, peckish, mustached, freckled, eye-patched love. It's all difficult.

All kinds of love.

"There's more than one fish swimming in the sea," Nana says on cue, but I know now that fish aren't the only thing swimming around.

"If you were a sea creature, what would you be?" I ask that

night at dinner. "A hermit crab? A manta ray? Maybe a beluga whale?"

It is a silly question, but she answers seriously.

"A sea cucumber," she says. "They are the least exciting."

Nana wants me to finish my soup. It's the alphabet kind. It will make me feel better.

I dangle my spoon in the broth, watching pasta letters bob and sink in a sea of language. Several of Roosevelt's New Deal agencies establish themselves, then dissipate. Otherwise, the soup's messages are spelled out in words I can't understand.

"You would make a good echinoderm," I say finally. Then I inform Nana of my plans to clean my room later that night. She seems pleased and offers to vacuum, once the floor is clear. I tell her I've also been considering an outing tomorrow afternoon, perhaps to the local supermarket or a gas station.

I tell her I've come up with my own aphorism. She lifts an eyebrow.

"There's no such thing as free love. Get it? Like economics—free lunch."

She gets it, or at least she puts down her soup spoon, pats my head, and tells me to always remember that I am something pretty special.

But I still feel strung out, loose, like a fish on land, or a girl on the moon, or a flower no one recognizes taking root in an unexpected place.

VFW Post 1492

In Istanbul, minarets hold up the sky like tent stakes. They loft it above mosque domes and the Bosphorus, above markets where kebab meat greases the air and shop owners cast their conversations: *Have a look? Guten morgen. Otkâ'de ste? Where you from?*

Jasper steers through the noise, his fingers entwined in Evelyn's. "Would you consider," he murmurs into her ear, "a belly dancing dress?"

Evelyn returns a crescent moon smile.

The city is piles of oranges and pomegranates ready to be pressed to pulp for cups of juice. A city of squeezing. It funnels men, robed and mustached, past yellow-haired girls, breasts mashed into camisoles, past a thousand eyes flung upon the streets.

Evelyn squeezes Jasper's hand.

They go to their room in a shabby pension. The Ochre Ox. It smells of incense and cat litter; the walls are carpeted. They sink down upon their bed just as the minarets outside awake, the cries of muezzins echoing exalted, unknowable. They make love listening. Prayers crawl across their skin and—despite the heat, the humid air—they shiver.

Sam pictures all this from his mother's house in Massachusetts. A two-bedroom ranch on the edge of North Adams. Usually he spends the day watching *Tiny Toon* reruns—they keep him calm—but not today. Not this whole week.

"Evelyn West," he hears his mother say. She's in the kitchen, talking on the phone, but her words bleed into the living room. "That's right—Sam and Jasper both—yes—yes—*I know*— apparently she's some kind of reporter."

All week Sam's mother has been calling her friends, her sisters. She tells them that her son—by which she means her noncrippled son, the successful son, the painter living abroad—has yet another gallery opening. But there's more! He had run into a girl he knew from high school "in Turkey of all places!"

Sam can't stand to listen any longer. He steers his motorized chair to his bedroom, its tires bumping over a lip of linoleum like the grinding tread of a tank.

Jasper and Evelyn stroll the scimitar slice of an estuary, their elbows brushing. Hers are bare, braceleted; his in a light cotton shirt.

(Sam sees it all—eyes closed, eyes open—he can't not see.)

"Bet you never guessed this would happen," says Evelyn. She snakes a lover's arm around Jasper, her bracelets jangling.

On the path ahead: dark-haired boys whistle after loose dogs sniffing a fisherman's feet.

"That what would happen?" says Jasper, feigning ignorance.

Evelyn gives him a little shove, and they both go quiet. Then they begin walking faster, as if outracing their own thoughts.

The fisherman snarls back at the dogs, "Airy fic, airy fic."

"What I mean—" Jasper starts to say, but Evelyn clutches his shoulder, pointing.

By the water's edge, a trio of women snaps photos, each one swathed in an inky black burqa. Only their eyes are exposed.

"When they take pictures," murmurs Evelyn, "do they tell each other to smile?"

Her breath lingers by Jasper's ear, warm and ripe, but he shakes the question off. "What I mean," he says, taking her soft stubby fingers, "is that I wasn't expecting anything to happen—between us—but I'm glad that—"

Evelyn lets out a hard little laugh. "What else would I do here? My job?"

She pulls away, but her cheeks go rosy.

(*Do they think of me?* Sam wonders, but even inside his own mind he feels forgotten.)

She's slimmer than she once was, but still a little pug-nosed. Still spiteful. In high school she'd been the new girl—arriving from Oklahoma just after the planes crashed—but everyone had other things to talk about. Everyone but them: a pair of twin brothers she followed around. They had talked about how to get rid of her. They'd even tried outright ignoring her. And yet, she continued asking them for rides, borrowing their CDs; a funny girl who knew how to pick a lock and swear in German. She was harmless, they'd eventually decided. She lightened the mood.

Besides, as brothers they'd believed themselves insoluble.

Evelyn's hair, newly sheared short as a boy's, gleams gold against her neck. She moves like a minnow through the crowd, her gold bracelets shimmering in the afternoon sun. When the city's minaret speakers erupt in prayer, Jasper can't help but catch her in his arms. It's become Pavlovian. When he hears the call to prayer, he has to kiss her.

Alone in his bedroom, Sam flicks a remote control. The TV turns on. He wants to block out the scene in his head; it has become too much to bear. He finds *Tiny Toons.* Dizzy Devil is blown up for the third time that day.

We're tiny, we're tooney, we're all . . .

Sam has no legs below the knee, a missing arm, a paralyzed

left side. When asked about serving in Iraq—the wounds that brought him home—he likes replying, "Being crippled is great! Retirement at twenty-four!" The response frightens people off. His aunts, the few old friends still entrenched around town. The same people who used joke of double vision when they saw him and his twin brother. Him and Jasper: both spindle-legged and flame-haired, running with synced strides around the infinite oval of their high school track.

Dizzy Devil gets pounded to a pancake with an oversized mallet, but Sam can't focus. Again, Istanbul wells up inside him, Jasper's senses overtaking his own. He feels Evelyn rake her fingers down his brother's back. He smells her salty heat. His skin goosebumps. His breath quickens.

You ever read each other's minds? Their friends used to ask. *You ever feel each other fall down—that's a twin thing right?*

They'd been serious types, him and Jasper. Pensive, with no interest in New Age hokum.

Don't be a dumbass, one of them would answer.

But now Sam knows better: he's got phantom limbs, just not his own. The indignity makes him laugh so hard he coughs up spittle. Same as he'd done a year ago, arriving home limp and full of stitches, arriving home cursing—*those Arab-motherfucker towelheaded bastards, those ungrateful sandniggers*—nearly asphyxiating himself on the force of his rage. Nearly but not quite. Another hilarious side effect of being trapped in a body as broken as his: suicide became much more difficult.

Not that he didn't still think about it. He thought about it all the time.

"You have an accident?" says his mother, hustling into his room with a laundry basket lodged against her hip. She wipes the spittle from his chin. She does this brusquely, though not unkindly. Sam does not say thank you.

Was it an accident? he wonders. An accident that he'd assumed Evelyn off limits?

"Samuel." His mother sets down her laundry basket, turns down the TV volume. "That man called again. The one from the VFW."

Sam can tell by his mother's tone that he's meant to respond.

"It isn't far." She smiles, exposing coffee-stained teeth, strained pink gums. "I could even take you this afternoon."

Sam says nothing. He would argue with her—he always argues with her—but today his mind is elsewhere; today, he feels his brother's hands undo the buttons on Evelyn's dress.

"Sam." His mother's smile wavers. "You haven't left the house in ages."

The buttons are silver, like the nursery rhyme. Cold.

"Well, if you have no objections, I'll get the van ready."

Hefting the laundry basket back onto her hip, his mother walks out of the room. Sam tries to concentrate on the blaze of color bubbling from the TV, but Jasper's fingers replace his own—the ones left lying bloody and mangled amid piles of trash and cement in Samawah—they slide up Evelyn's thighs and then inside her.

VFW Post 1492 is a dim but clean room, wood-paneled. Men sit in stiff metal chairs, clustered around a card table, their beer cans in cozies, their baseball caps embroidered, *US Air Force-Korea, 75th Ranger Regiment Vietnam, Steelers*—except one wearing a Santa hat. Inexplicable in mid-July.

"Welcome," calls out a Gulf War veteran—handsome despite his age—as Sam motors his wheelchair into the room. "We were just about to play rummy." The Gulf vet turns to the others, murmurs, "Josie McQuerrie's son."

The men nod. Their eyes wander all over Sam—across his pasty skin, his absent limbs—making him wish he'd tried harder to protest the trip. Usually, when people see him they glance away quickly. But not these men. They look directly at him, unashamed for looking. Unashamed for knowing what his body means.

It disturbs Sam: losing his little bit of mystery.

"Hey, you wanna doughnut?" calls one of the men. "We got a whole box. Seven flavors."

Sam tells the man no. He makes a study of the room's wood paneling.

"Suit yourself." The veterans return to their card game. Sam is surprised and almost disappointed when they don't press him further. He'd been all geared up for a fight. But soon enough, sitting quiet and alone, he is enveloped by the familiar steadiness of solitude.

For a limited time, buzzes a radio in a back corner, *only $19.95 . . .*

Sam doesn't stay comfortable for long. The VFW fades into a different scene—a room, heavily draped, the air thick and meaty—Jasper on a bed, prick hard; Evelyn twisting sheets into tourniquets around their limbs.

"You a'right?" calls a voice.

The man in the Santa hat waves his hands in front of Sam's face.

"Yeah," says Sam, embarrassed, but also repulsed. The Santa man has sour breath, a grating nasal voice.

"You get them—" The man thinks for a second, even twists himself into a cartoonish thinker pose, wrist bent under chin, "—you get them flashbacks? What's it? Pee tee ess dee?" The Santa man pulls up a chair, scoots closer, doughnut crumbs in his beard. "You can tell me, son. I got a reputation around here—a helper I am."

Sam glances toward the card table, hoping one of the others will notice the nutcase and drag him away. But all eyes are on the Gulf vet, who's exclaiming "Amen Charleston!" and waving a fistful of cards.

"It'll help me, helping you," presses the Santa man. "Come on, tell Uncle Danny. You get them flashbacks? They say talking's the best cure. What're you seeing son?"

Sam knows what he could say, what would make the guy happy. He could describe Samawah: the choking dust and the date palms and the Euphrates slugging along. He could say that he'd been a head-down-stay-out-of-trouble soldier—that he should have been fine. Low-level intelligence gathering, that was his job. He threaded through neighborhoods, an interpreter at his arm. *Do you feel safer since the invasion?* he asked bearded men, stiff and supplicating to his M-16. *Has your business been affected?* He spent thirteen months overseas and never got a scratch, then one day he paused in front of a barefoot boy selling tasseled hats. Sam had pointed to a hat and beckoned. A souvenir for his brother, he'd thought: a stupid thing they'd laugh about later. *Imayu thani,* said the boy, and then a car beside them had blown up.

Sam could say all this; he knows it's what the guy wants.

But his mouth won't form the words.

The Santa man leans in even closer, his face filling Sam's vision, the stink of his breath turning Sam's stomach. A few of the other vets finally look over. No one says anything. "Tell Uncle Danny." The Santa man's face has become wolfish, even mean. Sam leans backwards in his wheelchair as far as he can, which is not very far. The face moves closer. "Tell Uncle Danny," it says, exhaling an engulfing putrid fog.

"My brother." Sam's words come out like a cough.

The Santa man sits up. "What's that?" His mouth breaks into a sloppy grin, as if to congratulate a top student. "Your brother in the war with you?"

Sam shakes his head. The man's smile sags.

"My brother and I ran track."

"Oh?"

"In high school." Sam isn't sure what he's saying, or why, but at least the Santa man has moved away a little from his face, at least the stench of the man's breath has receded. "We ran races together and both finished at the same time."

"He's dead?"

"No."

The Santa man leans further back in his chair and folds his arms across his chest, looking perplexed. The man's confusion fortifies Sam. He feels stronger, as if he's pushing the man away with this story: a meaningless, stupid story. "My brother and I," Sam continues, rambling onward, "we were twins, identical, and hardly anyone could tell us apart. Even our own mother mixed us up sometimes, everyone did. Everyone except this almost-fat girl from Oklahoma. Evelyn. That was her name. Neither of us even really liked her. She just started hanging around one day and we couldn't get rid of her, we—"

To Sam's dismay, the Santa man grins, says, "I had some girlfriends once."

Sam can't help himself. "No!" he exclaims. "She wasn't a girlfriend, that was the whole point."

The Santa man stays silent, takes a swig of beer.

"Well maybe there was this one time—" Sam finds himself wishing, more than ever, that he could stand up and walk away. He feels lightheaded. The stink of bad breath has returned, again threatening to engulf him. Jasper's face—his own face—flickers through his vision. "There was this one time," repeats Sam, speaking faster. Rushing along. "Evelyn and I were waiting for Jasper in a movie theater parking lot. We were waiting in a pickup truck, waiting for Jasper to buy candy in a convenient store across the street. But then all of a sudden she reached over and unzipped my pants. Evelyn did. She did it without looking at me. She unzipped my pants and held my cock in her hand. Just held it and said nothing."

Sam gulps for air. He's panting, he discovers. The Santa man takes another swig.

"It wasn't a big deal," Sam croaks. "It wasn't. It really wasn't. Only lasted about a minute."

The Santa man leans back in his chair. He chews on his lip and squints at Sam. Finally he says, "'Bout what I expected."

Sam chokes up, realizing what he's just said. He hasn't thought of the story in years, having buried it beneath what followed: his newfound sense of singularity, invincibility. It wasn't long after the truck incident that he'd decided to enlist. The decision surprised everyone, his brother most of all—the brother with whom he'd spent countless nights imagining a future running track at UConn or Penn State. "Really?" Jasper had said. He'd looked at Sam, his face painted with wonderment, with hurt. "Why didn't you tell me?"

An argument flares up at the card table. "Just a minute," says the Santa man lurching to his feet, as if he'd been waiting for a reason to escape. "You sit tight."

Sam spends the remaining twenty minutes sitting alone. The radio gurgles and sings. Minutes move slow, the men's amicable bickering rising and falling like the break of distant waves. There's something airtight about the room, Sam decides. As if even time is trapped there. As if they were to go outside, any of them, they might dissolve and disappear.

His mom arrives at four o'clock.

"How was it?" she asks, after loading him and his wheelchair into the van.

Sam's instinct is to say nothing. Or to say something punishing, like: *Just leave me in a jail cell next time.*

Instead, he tells her it was fine. The answer catches them both off guard. Their eyes meet warily in the rearview mirror, and Sam sees her face slacken, as if the strings holding it up had been cut.

His mother looks away first. "No thundershowers today," she says, looking through the windshield toward blue sky. Her voice is a little hoarse.

Sam stares out the window as well, at houses flush with summer greenery, their vegetable gardens rowdy, doors thrown open. A weariness settles on him. He sees clumps of children sitting sweaty and bored on front steps, kicked outside to play, all of them waiting for something to happen: kids, fat-cheeked, bruised-kneed, wheeling flat-tired bicycles, licking popsicle juice off their knuckles, sensing so much more to come.

"Sam—" His mother blinks away the wetness around her eyes.

"It was fine," Sam says again, as if angry for having to repeat himself. But his usual gust of anger feels flaccid. Half-hearted. He looks in the rearview mirror once more, only sees his own face. It makes him flinch—his brokenness—how far he is from being healed. Closing his eyes, he sees the rounded glint of a mosque dome, tastes the ache of dusty air. He finds himself wondering, for the first time, if these sensations were really Jasper's. If they were ever Jasper's.

But how he wishes, how hard he wishes, that they were.

Jasper's eyes roam the dim street, searching for Evelyn. He stays up all night, pacing their room, peering out the pension window. She'd said she needed to go for a walk—that she needed some space—after he asked her to come live with him in his apartment in Berlin.

Across the street, two men pass cigarettes back and forth.

"Where are you?" breathes Jasper into the night. "Where have you gone?"

At dawn the sun daggers across Istanbul, illuminating the steady pulse of the Bosphorus, the city's bronze roofs. Old women stand in doorways, sowing seeds for pigeons. Men wheel tea carts to their posts.

When Evelyn slips into their room, she smells like cumin, like sumac and cinnamon. For several moments, she and Jasper look at one another as if from far away.

"I was going to tell you no way in hell," says Evelyn. "I really was."

She lifts her dress over her head and lies down upon the bed. Jasper lies down beside her, and for a long time they do not touch. Then he traces his finger across the blank canvas of her body. Outside the window, a young man starts to sing.

Later, they sleep, their breaths aligned, and when Jasper awakes, the air hums with cumin, sumac, and cinnamon. He finds himself unable to move, astonished by what has passed, paralyzed by it: the sheer horror, the ecstasy of being alive.

Bury Me

Beware the pine-tree's withered branch!
Beware the awful avalanche!
—HENRY WADSWORTH LONGFELLOW

———————

It was the strangest funeral I'd ever attended. Sun-soaked—on the old farm field behind Sally's house—the bereaved dressed in a rainbow of colors, the air sugared with cotton candy and the pangs of a string quartet. A downy white pony for children to ride.

Sally saw me and came sailing across the lawn, a loose yellow dress lashed to her body.

"My mother's," she said, hiking the dress past her knees, as if she were a little girl crossing a mud puddle. "I'm so glad you're here." She gave me a wet, splintering smile. "I almost thought you weren't coming."

"Sal—"

But already she was gone, engulfed by relatives, all of them echoes of her: lithe Nordic bodies, white-blond hair, long noses. Polished people who looked like they'd be cold to touch.

I had not wanted to come. It had been three months since I'd so much as grabbed coffee with Sally, and in those months, I'd finally felt able to think straight. "It's my work," I'd told her, in the phone calls I answered. "I'm unbelievably busy." I said this, despite living less than two hours away. Despite the fact that her mother was dying—for real this time, no more chance of remission— and that her father had been dead for eight years. I deliberately took on extra hours, extra projects, anything to stay longer in the white light of the lab, among whirring fans, trays of bladderwort and daffodils standing erect in the place where I believed myself happy.

Notes 4/12 — Characteristics
Native to New England, Pinus Strobus *is also known as White Pine, Soft Pine, and Weymouth Pine. The evergreen tree takes a conical shape. Fast growing, given the proper climate.*

"Madeleine," called a voice, and I peered out toward the other funeral attendees, like bright dashes of paint dotting the lawn. No sign of Sally. No sign that the voice belonged to anyone. A caterer lunged at me with a tray of little marzipan animals: zebras, penguins, a slumping chimpanzee. I felt dizzy.

"Madeleine."

I turned to find Lou Crane, one of Sally's ex-boyfriends (always Lou Crane, never Lou. "Like Charlie Parker," he used to tell people). He'd gotten paunchy since college but still had the same foxy, glittering eyes. He beckoned from a half circle of young men, some of whom looked familiar. More of Sally's ex-boyfriends, I realized.

It surprised me, seeing them, though it shouldn't have. Sally had the uncanny ability to stay close after breakups. The boyfriends waved, a few hugged me—they all seemed to be getting along quite well—unaware, evidently, of their own oddity: a series of successive upgrades, each in turn abandoned.

"So," said Lou Crane, as he and the other boyfriends dismantled a tray of blue cheese canapés. "I got us some stuff for tonight." He exaggerated the word *stuff*.

"Tonight?" I echoed.

"We're having a party."

In college, Lou Crane had called himself a musician—played saxophone and wore his hair long—but even then you could detect a harshness, a bulldoggedness, beneath the smell of hash. How fitting that he'd since started working in finance.

"For Sally," he added, drawing close, "to take her mind off things."

Despite the circumstances, I had enjoyed seeing Lou Crane—enjoyed jostling shoulders with my past—but now I wanted to shut that past out. I wanted to return to my clear-eyed life: the 6:00 A.M. jogs, the hissing cappuccino maker, a newspaper so fresh it smudged my palms black.

"Can't stay," I said, trying to sound disappointed. "Got to get back—work."

Lou Crane gave me a *come on* look, the other boyfriends following his gaze, as if it were a road leading from him to me. "Maddy," he said, like he owned the name. He looked at me, eyes brimming with remembrance, with the authority of having once watched me crawl across a frat room floor, of having once walked in on me blowing his roommate (I'd flipped him off and kept going), of having, perhaps more than anyone, witnessed the nights Sally and I seemed to float untouchable, reckless to the point of elegance.

"I think it would mean a lot to her if you stayed." The voice belonged to one of the other boyfriends, one I hadn't noticed at first. Carlton, I guessed. Sally's current beau. He wore a well-tailored jacket and had large, clean-looking hands. "She talks about you so often," he added, with the sort of sincerity I might have mocked in other circumstances. He was the kind of guy Sally and I had both avoided in college.

"What d'you think?" asked Lou Crane again, and, in the presence of Carlton, I felt a moment of allegiance. Maybe I could handle one night—just one—for the sake of the girl I'd once called my best friend. One night and I'd drive home in the morning.

But even thinking this, my mouth went dry; I felt the breath siphoned from my lungs.

Notes 4/12 — Growth Patterns
White Pine seeds distributed by wind. Cone production peaks every three to five years, with two years required for full maturity.

The funeral service was about to begin. The cotton candy machine was silenced, the pony held fast. Everyone gathered around a gazebo covered in ribbons and balloons. A passerby might have thought we were assembling for a birthday party or an unconventional wedding if all the brightly dressed people hadn't looked so grave.

"Planned the whole thing on her deathbed," I overheard a woman tell the man at her elbow.

"She would, wouldn't she," the man answered. He might have said more, but their pious incredulity drifted out of earshot.

I had not known Sally's mother well. She visited campus only once or twice. An elegant woman, even with skin turned waxy from chemo, hair fallen away. And yet it had been her idea to get drunk on margaritas with Sally and me in a dive bar three towns over. Drunk enough for us to sing bad renditions of "Baby One More Time," Sally's mother singing loudest of all, her bald head gleaming under neon lights. Even with the trappings of old New England money, she—like her daughter—had never been a stuffy woman.

That, or she had been a woman who always liked to get her way.

As the funeral got started, I found a seat apart from the boyfriends and most of the guests. I sat with my back against a tree, ignoring the root prodding my hip, the snag of bark. From there, I could see Sally. She sat near the microphone, yellow dress draped over her chair, hands folded in her lap. I tried to imagine how I'd arrange my face if she turned around and looked at me. I decided I would give her a strong smile, whatever that meant.

People spoke. The sunshine became heavy. Sally did not turn around, and I began wondering if I should speak. The facilitator was welcoming people up for a sort of open mic. This was something I could do, I realized, something I could do for Sally. She had not spoken herself. She was an outgoing person but hated public speaking. They called again for the open mic. The offer tickled my throat. I couldn't move—I was there for Sally, not her mother.

It was only Sally I could eulogize:

How unfortunate, we used to say, that the two of us weren't born lesbians.

How unlucky.

Sally and I, we met in an astronomy class both of us eventually dropped, but our connection, we decided, had always been in the stars. We could finish each other's sentences on the first day. By the second week we'd already mapped out our whole life: us, together after college in the farmhouse she'd inherit. There'd be yoga at sunrise, baskets of homegrown strawberries, stray cats, foreign lovers who flew in for weekends. We'd learn to sculpt, to play the accordion. We'd host outdoor concerts that would last for days.

This is what we used to tell each other, even as we both stood peering into a bar's bathroom mirror, coating our mouths with lipstick, painting our eyes. The visions of our future like a lullaby before we slipped into darkness.

She was a wonderful girl, Sally. A special girl.

I'll miss her.

"Where you off to?" said Lou Crane, catching sight of me when the service was over. I had assumed no one would notice if I left early. Everyone was struggling to stand, stunned by the weight of their grief, half-blind in the sunshine, in the confusion of ribbons and music. The band had started playing again. A little girl released a balloon.

I ignored Lou Crane and kept walking toward my car. I would send Sally a card, I'd decided. I would tell her I was sorry I hadn't been able to stay longer.

"Hey," said Lou Crane, jogging after me and grabbing my shoulder. "Hey, don't walk away." His grip became insistent. Knowing him, I couldn't help wondering if this was all part of some half-assed scheme to sleep with me.

"Let go," I said, tugging myself free, preparing to tell him off. But when I looked at his face again, the foxiness was gone. Instead I saw a strained gaze, pupils rimmed with white. Of course he still cared for Sally. They all did, all those boys. They were each here to save her.

Well, I told myself, *then let them save her.*

"Please stay." Lou Crane reached for me again. "She needs you, she—"

As he spoke, I realized what he, what all of them, thought I could do. He thought that with my history—the history I shared with Sally—I could give the girl a night of oblivion. A few hours, at least, of forgetting.

"I can't, I—"

Too late: the shrill birdcall of my name, the flash of a yellow dress.

"You ready to paar-tay?" Sally draped an arm on each of my shoulders, so that for a moment her face eclipsed my whole vision. Oval and bone pale. She raised an eyebrow, meaning to be salacious, but the movement only made her appear more unhinged. It made me want to hide her. To put her away where she wouldn't be seen by anyone, by me.

"Madeline was just heading to her car," said Lou Crane. He gave me a dirty look, but I felt grateful that he had said it and not me.

Sally, though, appeared unfazed. In fact, she grinned and said, "Of course, Maddy was just going to grab her sleeping bag." Then she drew even closer, all earth smells and bright blond hair, running her hands down my arms, pausing at my wrists, manacling them with her thin cold fingers. "Right, babe?"

"Actually—" I murmured, but Sally sprang away.

"The house is all ours tonight," she exclaimed with steely joy. "We're going to have so much fun. It's been so long since I had any fun." She looked at me, at the boyfriends who had begun gathering around. "No parents, no rules!" She was trying to make a joke, but none of us laughed. Sally waited for a moment, then laughed for us, her voice clanging like a warning bell. Her mouth the darkest hole.

Notes 4/12—Potential Problems
Threats to Pinus Strobus *include Blister Rust, and the White Pine Weevil, as well as strong winds, heavy snowstorms, and air pollution.*
The tree, however, is relatively resistant to fire.

With the funeral guests packed away and gone, the night closing in, the boyfriends and I stood in Sally's kitchen taking small
sips of whiskey. Sally gulped. We passed around a joint, mainly
passing it to her. The boyfriends looked pleased. She was changing, we could all see that; she was blossoming, color coming into
her cheeks, eyes sparkling.

Lou Crane clinked his glass with Carlton's. Everyone seemed
to relax.

Then, without warning, Sally dropped to the floor. She rolled
around for a moment, then began punching and kicking the air,
blond hair thrashing, her face smeared with tears. The boyfriends
stepped back, scared to touch her. They looked at me as if I might
do something. It made me want to laugh, their scared faces. *It's
just Sally*, I wanted to say. *What did you expect?*

I knelt beside her so that she flailed against me for a moment
before going still. Then I eased myself down onto the floor and
into her arms. Sally had kept her eyes closed, but now she opened
them. "Remember," she said to me, still catching her breath, "remember the dean's lawn?"

"Oh, I remember," I replied, my solemnity giving her a little
spasm of giggles. "We peed on it."

She went on like this for a while, remembering things while
the boys stood stiff and silent around us. "The Goat Room," she'd
say. Or "poker night!" And I'd nod, then add flesh to the memory:
remind her of how we'd filled the Goat Room with candles and
nearly burnt the place down. How one poker night we'd won all
her math tutor's clothes. Or even better: our double date with a
pair of lacrosse players—star athletes, campus studs—whom we'd
ditched five minutes into the winter formal to watch *Casablanca*
in my room.

It was a strange feeling, recounting those stories. A tingling
feeling. Almost like recognizing myself in photographs I'd forgotten I was in.

Eventually, Sally and I got up and started drifting through the
house, from room to room. I don't know what happened to the
boys. They didn't matter anymore; I convinced myself they had
never mattered. As we drifted, Sally touched objects—a tall glass
lamp, her mother's quilt—as if they were new to her.

"Remember," she said, "our wedding?"

She picked up a photo frame, held it to me, and I saw us: decked out in frothy white thrift-store dresses, holding hands on the college quad. It had been her idea, our sophomore year. By that time her mother's cancer still could have gone either way, but Sally wasn't taking any chances. "I want a wedding photo for my mother," she'd said, "and you're my one true love." So we held a ceremony on the quad, and some nearby Frisbee players officiated. A passing tour group stopped to watch. "You may kiss the other bride," our makeshift priest declared, and we'd made out like we sometimes did at parties, sloppily, half giggling, tongues sliding on teeth, loving how we could shock people.

After that, we'd honeymooned in the cafeteria.

"I wish," said Sally, "I'd kept that dress."

We were in the living room by then, on the couch. A tangle of limbs. I couldn't remember getting there. All around us: funeral bouquets. Bright bunches of white lilies. Lilacs, her mother's favorite. Azaleas. All piled in the room.

"It's been so good to see you," Sally murmured, nuzzling my arm.

Her words made my heart pound. This is what I'd feared most— her needing me more than I needed her—the moment when I'd have to explain that.

"Sally," I said. "Sally, the thing is—"

She placed a finger on my lips. "Shhh," she said. "Enough talking."

So we lay together, inhaling the flowers—their painful perfume, their last gasps—until a figure loomed over us: Carlton, announcing that it was late, that it was time for bed, as he scooped Sally up in his arms.

"No," Sally moaned, dizzy with tiredness. But even as she said it, she pressed herself against him.

"No," I echoed.

Toward the end of college, when I started retreating more often to the library, even staying until close on Friday and Saturday nights, Sally used to visit me. She'd come by, dressed for a party: short skirt, skin peppered with glitter, feet jammed into heels. By that time her mother's health was only getting worse, but that was never what she wanted to talk about.

"Plants," she'd say, perched on the end of my desk and making a little pout. "Tell me what you love so much about plants."

And I'd answer, "You don't really want to hear this," but she'd nod, her earrings tinkling, and say, "Yes, I really do." So, sighing, I would tell her about Hawaiian mosses that had been cloning themselves for five thousand years. About the corpse flower that smells like rotting meat. Or the famous kadupul blossom, blooming only at night and withering before dawn. And I'd get carried away. I'd realize other people were looking up from their books, glaring over at me, but that Sally was still listening; she was trying so hard to listen. And that's when I'd start to feel angry. Angry, I told myself, that she could never understand why I needed to study so much. Growing up, I'd had to fight my way through public schools for scholarships. I couldn't just graduate with good grades, I needed the best grades. How could that make sense to her? There was a building on campus named after her family.

But of course, my anger was never really for Sally. And, if I'd been honest with myself, I wasn't even that desperately poor.

The morning after the funeral, sunlight lanced through windows in dusty rays. The boyfriends lay sprawled asleep on couches and easy chairs, Lou Crane's chainsaw snores concealing the creak of stairs as I crept toward Sally's room. I'd woken clearheaded, resolute: I would invite Sally to stay with me. I would invite her down for the weekend, take her out for dinner, maybe even show her around the lab. The idea made me feel giddy, openhearted. This would be a fresh start for our friendship. A new chapter.

Upstairs, Sally lay on her bed next to Carlton, who still wore his clothes from the night before. Sally, though, was naked. It was how she liked to sleep. I had seen her naked plenty of times, but never so still. Never like that. It shocked me—the vulgarity of nude flesh—her flat chest, hipbones jutting forward, pubic hair shaved away. There was nothing I couldn't see.

Sally opened her eyes.

"Oh," I said, hastily looking away, then back again. "I'm leaving. I have to go."

Sally rolled languidly toward me. "Okay, bye," she said, yawning, her eyelids already fluttering closed, her breaths returning to long, easy measures.

Her words—or lack of words—stunned me. I remained unmoving, unable to believe our conversation could end there, that it could end so quickly, that she would let me leave.

"Sally," I whispered. My hand hovered above her body. Two inches, maybe less. I wondered what it would mean to touch the white plane of her skin, what it would have meant, those years ago, to have crossed the threshold on the far side of friendship. "What a shame we weren't born lesbians," we used to say. And we'd meant it.

"Sally," I whispered again, this time a little louder.

We had loved each other, hadn't we? It had been a difficult kind of love—the kind that always stops short of fulfillment—but it had been love, nonetheless.

"Sal, wake up."

Carlton groaned and stretched, one arm falling across Sally's chest.

I fled. I tumbled back through the house, past the boyfriends just beginning to stir. Lou Crane called out to me, but I pushed through the front door, out into the dazzle of a summer morning, gasping for air, choking on the realization that Sally hadn't been trying to pin me down or keep me in her life. She'd been trying to say goodbye.

Notes 4/12—Mechanisms for Survival

"But really," Sally had giggled in the library, even when I made an exasperated point of looking at my watch, made it clear there wasn't much else to say. We were close to finals, to graduation, and every minute felt precious: another drop of water, swallowed or lost. "Why?" said Sally, twirling her hair. "Why do you love plants so much?"

So I told her, in excruciating detail, about abscission. I had my botany textbook open—a section on white pine—and I pointed to an image of the tree. *Foliage includes fascicles of five bluish green needles.* I told her how the plant would sometimes drop part of itself. *Abscission typically occurs in the colder months.* That it would excise its needles, its cones, even an entire branch in order to make the whole stronger. *This process of detachment furthers chances for survival.*

When I finished and looked at Sally again, there was something wrong with her face. Usually she listened with an expression of vague dreaminess, a smile lolling on her lips, but at that moment, she showed complete understanding. Understanding mixed with something I couldn't quite place. It almost looked like pity.

I still think of that moment as I unwind hours in the lab, grinding plants down to their most essential parts, unlocking their secrets in the march of retrogression and reassembly. Chymopapain. Taxol. Podophyllotoxin. It makes me feel like a magician, an alchemist—though I'd never admit so to my colleagues—to find and conjure these substances from the paper thinness of a leaf, the frailty of a petal. It's hard to explain, but sometimes I still believe I could find anything.

Syndication

My parents are in the backyard, digging their ♡
graves. I'm in the kitchen with Orange, my younger brother, and
we're watching through a grubby little window. My parents work
without speaking. They are not fit people, but they do not stop
for breaks. Sweat blooms under their armpits and around their
bandanas.

The graves are being dug next to the outhouse, and are approaching six feet by four feet by three feet.

That's how I know they aren't for us.

Still, I decide it would be best to keep Orange from watching,
so I suggest we play one of our favorite games: Prank Call! It's

where we dial random numbers and pretend to be debt collectors. Sometimes we pretend to be hookers too. Or long lost children.

Orange wraps his sticky fingers around the phone receiver, forehead pleating into focus. His tongue lolls out of his mouth like a fat pink slug. He's an ugly kid—but he doesn't know that yet—which makes me love him even more.

"Broked." Orange looks at me, confused.

I press the phone against my ear and listen for a dial tone.

"Broked," I echo.

Through the window we hear the dirt-gnaw of shovels: the scrape and thump, scrape and thump.

I know I should be full of fearing, but instead I feel a sense of lightness—a birthday party feeling—like anything could happen and it's my day to choose.

"Put your rain boots on," I tell Orange, even though the sky is clear and it's been the hottest August ever.

Orange doesn't argue. Besides failing to notice his own ugliness, he hasn't yet discovered he's allowed to say no, which is also something I like about him, most of the time.

While Orange gets his rain boots, I hear a new sound: a hush-hush sound. I peer out the kitchen window and see two rectangular holes. Two shovels propped against the outhouse.

I do not see our parents.

Orange comes up beside me, his eyes as wide as soup bowls.

"Look," I say, and point toward two quails tottering across the yard. "Our parents have turned into birds."

I'm joking, of course, but Orange skitters through the kitchen and out the front door, hollering at the quails until they go goosing into the sky.

I run out after him. Now I'm scared, just like the quails, by all the noisiness after quiet. I grab Orange's hand and keep running. The two of us careen across the yard, plunging into the forest that surrounds our house like a leafy overcoat—trees in every direction—except for a single narrow road, like a dirt zipper.

Orange and I crash and bump and skin our knees, and we go from cold-sweat-scared to laugh-leaping and collapsing in a heap of giggles and blood in the mossy nook of a pine tree.

"Hey, you got a light?" says Orange, which is something he must have heard on TV.

I pantomime taking a lighter out of my dress pocket, and then we both smoke imaginary cigars.

"Where can a guy get a drink around here?" murmurs Orange, already half-fallen asleep.

I put a piece of moss under his head. Then I put a piece of moss under my head and close my eyes and imagine both of us being hugged tight and warm by a huge fur coat, its pockets full of cough drops and unused handkerchiefs.

When we wake, the sun has sunk low enough to stab sideways through trees. It's the time of day our parents usually come trundling up the dirt road in their truck and we all sit down in front of the TV and Mom massages Dad's feet and I massage my own feet, and sometimes Orange's feet, until Dad calls me a little perv.

Orange and I both wake up stiff, so we start walking through the woods in no particular direction. I can tell Orange is hungry because I'm hungry too. Neither of us says anything, though, because we're too busy seeing our parents everywhere. We see a pair of squirrels chattering at us from a tree branch. Then two stumps, mossy and indignant. Two beams of light.

Orange shivers because he's only wearing rain boots and a diaper. He's potty trained, but he prefers the feel, he says—it's like a butt pillow—and Mom said that was fine because it meant less laundry.

I pull off my dress and give it to him. The dress drags around his ankles, but he's careful not to trip. Now I'm just in my undies and sandals. It makes me feel strong, being mostly naked. I don't feel cold. I give Orange another imaginary cigar.

The last dribbles of daylight leak from the forest, and Orange and I begin bumping into things. The bumping is almost fun, though, and I start to get the birthday party feeling again. I start believing things could go on like this—like it might always be me and my brother on an adventure—like it might always be my day to choose.

Except then we catch sight of a lamp-lit window.

Orange and I slide up to the house like ghosts, or arsonists. Or like two children who've always longed to discover another house out in the woods away from their doomsday-prepping bandana-wearing parents, but who are also nervous now that they've found it. Orange nearly trips on the hem of my dress and makes a squeaking sound. We both freeze, but nothing happens. An open window, square as a TV frame, pours out light. We slip our heads up over the windowsill, chins on the ledge, because at night it's always easier to in-look than out-look.

And we look. We drink in this other life.

After a few minutes, though, I slide my chin off the windowsill. I've realized that I've seen this show before—I know what will happen—and it makes me feel proud and sad at the same time: my knowing.

Orange keeps watching, his big ugly grin lit by the window-glow.

I start massaging his feet. I do this until we both feel a gentle kind of happy.

For now, no one tells me to stop.

The
Future
Consequences
of Present
Actions

When a boy wakes, he must not make a sound. He must kneel beside his bed in silent prayer, like the others in the room, and feel the weight of two minutes. He must feel joy too. And gratitude. If such sensations do not arise, a boy must report this to his Caretaker. A boy must strip his bed. He must fold his bedclothes lengthwise and lay them flat across two chairs, a pillow on each seat. A boy must dress in trousers. A frock. A vest. The vest must be fashioned from coarse cotton and must be blue or white, never an extravagant color, especially not red. A boy must comb his hair. Clean his teeth. A boy must not spit on the floor—this is a vulgar act. All spitting should be directed toward the spit box. A boy must take his turn carrying the slop bucket out into a morning still dark and trembling with the groans of milk-heavy cows. A boy must not spill. If a spill occurs, a boy must not make vulgar pronouncements. Vulgar pronouncements include "hang it" and "plague on it." A boy must report all such phrases to his Caretaker. He must change into clean trousers, a clean frock and vest. The essentiality of cleanliness cannot be overstated. A boy must hurry to breakfast, for punctuality is likewise indispensable. At breakfast, he must kneel again in silence. Two minutes. A boy must eat with the other boys. His table must be one in a long row of tables, set with bone-white crockery, the dishes grouped by four to reduce the need for passing. A boy must first eat what appeals to him least—the thick porridge—and then proceed to tastier morsels—the apple slices—and he must completely clear his plate. A boy must remember the feeling of a stomach pitted hollow by hunger. Fingers so cold they feel they will snap. A boy must sit still. He must not swivel his neck to search the faces of the others. He must not look for his father. If he finds himself doing so, he should report this to his Caretaker. A boy must be amenable. He must concede. He must not look for his father.

Charles Lane has always believed in the perfectibility of man. Always he has considered himself a voluntaryist, an abolitionist. He has abstained from meat, despite having butchers for brothers. An Englishman, aged a stately forty-six, he'd come to America because America—so hopeful and fertile and vast—seemed the place to start society anew.

This he tells the gray-eyed men in gray-blue shirts, the gray-eyed women in starched white dresses, all seated and staring from a dozen benched rows. All gathered together to judge him—his commitment to their cause.

And that of the boy at his side. His son, William Lane. Nervous as a cricket.

The gray-eyed take their time deciding. They are famous, world over, for their utter devotion to prudence. Their attentiveness to detail. The United Society of Believers, they call themselves. Outsiders know them as the Shakers. For Charles Lane, they are his second chance: another stab at earthly paradise.

"Brother," says a gray-eyed man. He rises, slow as winter wheat, from his place on a bench in the assembly hall. "Do you feel prepared to sever all your worldly ties?"

Charles Lane feels the bite of desperation. Two years he has lived in America, years he'd wasted on a transcendental goose hunt: funding a utopian experiment beset by freeloaders, by a family—the Alcotts—who praised communal living, yet who could not see beyond themselves.

Fruitlands they'd called their hapless commune. As if a ripe new Eden might have appeared in Massachusetts, born only of yearning.

"I am prepared to sever all ties," says Charles Lane with well-rehearsed conviction. It's true he feels at home within the confines of the Shaker village, at ease among the tidy orchards, the pastures ringed by fence posts planted deep as spears. And what restraint the people show! What prudent innovation! Just beyond the assembly hall stands a stone barn built in concentric circles for ventilating hay. Lodgings with windows installed at an angle to welcome in more light. Each room swept clean. Everywhere the smell of bread. Everyone well-rested and solemn. These people do not proselytize, and yet their numbers swell even in the absence of progeniture. Merchants, midwives, students, and soldiers now among them. Methodists. Baptists. Roman Catholics. Jews.

"You have no wife?"

Charles Lane sits pinned by the gaze of a gray-eyed woman, her face shadowed by a plain white bonnet. He clears his throat. He is not a man of the flesh, he tells her, though he uses many more words—words that wander back to England, Greavesian ideology, his staunch belief in abstinence—before returning to the present moment: the little son beside him, back erect against a wooden chair, feet dangling above the polished floor. Little William. His father's greatest source of pride. His father's greatest source of shame.

"It is with the utmost conviction," says Charles Lane, this time addressing the whole assembly, "that I hold biological love to have a deleterious effect on the greater pursuit of a Universal Family."

He trembles as he speaks, thinking again of the Fruitlands commune, of those indulgent transcendentalists. Swindlers of his time and money! Though, admittedly, also admirably persuasive—

Beyond the narrow island of selfishness lies the continent of all-embracing love.

Those were Bronson Alcott's words, in the commune's early days. The summer days when blackberries ornamented woodlands and talk of Herodotus echoed through the kitchen. The days when visitors came and spoke of staying. When Bronson's envisioned continent still seemed within reach.

But the winds are not always propitious, and steam is only a recent invention.

How quickly Bronson's homely wife, Abigail, had begun favoring her own children: giving them treats, encouraging poems. And all at the commune's expense. At his expense! Charles Lane would never act so selfishly; he would never undermine his son's chance to participate in ventures greater than himself.

"Brother?" says the gray-eyed woman.

It was the Alcotts' love for their own blood that had spoiled the young utopia.

"Brother?" says the gray-eyed man.

Charles Lane returns to the assembly hall, the unblinking faces, and beyond them—out the polished windows—the lawns kept litterless even as maple trees shed their crimson autumn coats.

"I am prepared," says Charles Lane, "to take upon myself the cross."

The bonnets nod. The bearded give their chins a stroke.

"You have no debts?"

"Nay."

"You have no doubts?"

Charles Lane moves to sign the papers the gray-eyed men and women set before him. His eyes skim over "indentureship" and "William Lane" and "I will not take away the Said Children nor Control them." His mind has plunged ahead to a life unburdened by cupidity, the prejudices of lineage. A life restrained and orderly, conducted in the spirit of a Universal Family. With the whisk of the quill pen, he feels his past absolved. His future blooms. Thrumming with the buoyancy of the newly saved, Charles Lane turns to clutch his son, kiss the boy's forehead, but little William is being led away.

When entering a house, a boy must uncover his head and hang his hat on a peg and wipe his boots on the foot scraper. He must shut the door gently behind him. If the door is slammed, a boy must step back outside, reenter, and close the door again. A boy must fear God. A boy must learn the teachings of Mother Ann, God rest her soul. He must learn that God is both a man and a woman and that Mother Ann, God rest her soul, was the second coming of Christ in female form. He must recognize the inherent equality of the sexes. That celibacy is the path to eternity. *Do all your work as if you had a thousand years to live.* Industriousness is revelatory. *And as if you knew you must die tomorrow.* A boy must welcome other boys: the boys, like him, from foreign shores, the colored boys and orphans, the broke farmhands. A boy must be willing to share in all things. He must have no private property. This includes a marred daguerreotype of one's mother, God rest her soul. *Private property puts the devil in you.*

Elder Geary lets his body relax onto his cot: the wasted shoulders, the skull as bald and spotted as a farmyard egg. Around him, half a dozen Shaker Brethren have gathered to watch him die. The infirmary windows are open wide, despite the chill, to lessen his moribund stink. The Brethren are dry-eyed and thoughtful.

"I should like to see the children outfitted with new boots before winter," says Elder Geary.

"New boots before winter," echo the Brethren—except for one, who moves toward the window, pinching his nose.

For a moment, Elder Geary does not know the man: lean-limbed, thin-lipped, eyes as busy as mice. A stranger? An angel of death? Then he recalls the English neophyte—Charles Lane—arrived some months ago, along with his single son.

"It would be wise . . ." Elder Geary falters on his words. He cannot help staring at Charles Lane, who, he now recalls, had proven a satisfactory laborer, well-behaved, but who had yet to bequeath the Shaker coffers all his worldly assets.

He needed more time, Charles Lane had told them, to make arrangements.

A feeble excuse for a purported Believer.

"Brother?" The Brethren step a little closer, peer down into the old man's cot.

Charles Lane creeps closer as well, mouth-breathing. "Such an exemplary soul," he says of Elder Geary, his voice nasally and righteous. "He will be welcomed in the Kingdom of Heaven."

Elder Geary shudders. He feels a sweet drowsiness encroaching yet cannot justify succumbing. What would Mother Ann think, witnessing her teachings so desecrated? Many years ago, Elder Geary had followed the woman on her holy tour through Massachusetts—he'd heard her sing without words, heal without touch—and her principles of common property had galvanized his thumping heart. All Shakers, rich or poor, pooled their possessions so that all might aspire toward godliness. And yet this man, this Charles Lane, saw himself as an exception?

Elder Geary sits bolt upright.

The attending Brethren lurch back from his cot.

"Hear me!" Elder Geary lifts a shaking hand to point at Charles Lane. "We have an unbeliever among us."

The Englishman pales, then offers the Brethren a creaky smile, as if the accusation had come in jest. "Elder Geary is delirious," he says. "The deathbed muddle, for I—"

"An unbeliever!" Elder Geary's voice rings far louder than it has in years, loud enough to escape the open window and infuse the falling snow. Throughout the village, fellow Shakers pause their daily chores. Drop brooms and washbuckets. Look toward the sky. "Our sacred order, our blessed order, has a holy task." Elder Geary thinks again of Mother Ann: that blue-eyed woman so small in stature yet limitless in spirit. "We must separate the true believers from those living in sin."

Spent of the words that had held him upright, Elder Geary falls back upon his cot. The room begins to darken. His senses fade. And yet, even halfway to eternity, Elder Geary hears himself echoed:

". . . from those living in sin."

A boy must remember it is a privilege to be brought up among people of God, that beyond these grounds are the beggarly elements. The ravages of Babylon. To secure salvation, a boy must put his hands to work. His heart to God. He must learn to fashion brooms from bales of straw, and sieves from beechwood planks, and large oak casks to store molasses. He must learn to plant seeds. Pick apples. Drive a team of oxen. He must not give an ox a human name, however. This leads to wickedness. If a boy does give an ox a human name—perhaps Louisa—and kisses its snout and addresses it like a confidante, despite all instructions otherwise, he must discover that he will not be struck by rod or cane. He must discover, only, the disappointment of his fellow Shakers. Their heart-wrung sighs. Eyes cast toward heaven, their prayers for his soul. He must remember his father's bidding. He must remember that this is what his father chose.

"You are in need of assistance?" The voice belongs to a woman, a schoolteacher, a Miss Sophia Foord. She bids her driver slow his horses, pause beside a man flagging them from the bank of a waterlogged road. Not far beyond she sees his coach in muddy disarray: axle splintered, reins tangled where the horses bolted free.

"My sincerest thank you," says the man—wide-eyed and effusive—as if rescued from the bowels of a beasty wilderness and not merely poor luck on an otherwise fine spring day. A reaction made even odder, thinks Miss Foord, by the looming bulk of a Shaker stone barn about a mile to the west. Walking distance, no doubt.

Normally, Miss Foord would avoid such interruptions, but the day is crisp and bright and vernal, with sky-blue puddles jeweling the road, and she feels plucky, venturesome and wild.

"Sincerely grateful," says the man again, even bowing slightly. "My coachman ran off." He points toward a ridge, nut-brown and raw from winter, horse and human tracks braiding up its side. "I suspect—"

"Why, sir," interrupts Miss Foord, leaning from her coach window to study his face, "are you not one Charles Lane, associate of that good man Bronson Alcott?"

Charles Lane sheds his grateful countenance. "I suppose," he mutters, "you could say that."

"How propitious!" Miss Foord claps her hands. Her driver coughs, loudly, but she ignores him. "I heard your lecture in Boston—such astonishing ideas—the commune, what was it called? Berryfield? Fruitfarm? Fruitlands! I very nearly joined the whole endeavor!"

Charles Lane's scowl begins to melt. He stands a little straighter. "Ah yes," he says, "Bronson and I were on our Penniless Pilgrimage. We—"

"But where are you headed?" Miss Foord nods at his broken coach, its cabin shuttered by curtains. "The Alcott's have set up a lovely little cottage, and I"—she pauses, projects a modest blush—"I am on my way to serve as tutor to their daughters. The family would be delighted to see you—and your son, of course."

At "son," Charles Lane stiffens.

"Well, that's settled then. You both will ride with me. There's plenty of room." Miss Foord says this brightly. It is her personal theory that a woman's sanguinity—when adequately applied—can prove a formidable force. She smiles at Charles Lane, standing tense as a sapling beside the muddy road. *Men and their pride*, she thinks. She is not one to flirt, but today she feels a touch mischievous. Lowering her voice so that the driver cannot hear, she says, "If there exists bad blood between you and the Shaker people, we will all understand. They are such dreary company."

"It's not—"

"And if you're worried about your son's education, fear not!" Miss Foord claps her hands again, elated by her role in reuniting two distinguished men. "I'll be instructing the Alcott daughters in manifold subjects. Such savvy creatures—Louisa especially—and your son is more than welcome to join. Remind me his name?"

Charles Lane stares at her blankly.

The driver coughs again, rustles the horses' reins.

Miss Foord feels her excitement grow a little heavy. She looks again at the broken coach, its curtains fluttering in the breeze. "Sir?"

If a boy leaves the house to attend school or meals or meetings, he must go with a Brother, and they must walk two abreast and synchronized, always starting with their right feet first. Neither may speak. A boy must never visit a Sister's quarters, except for errands—and then only for fifteen minutes. When speaking with a Sister, a boy must say "agreeable things about nothing." He must not, under any circumstances, bring up the idea of departing from the Shakers. He must not bring up reasons why others have departed. Others include his father, whom he must not consider his father, but rather a man beset by sin. If a boy remains uncertain what to say, silence is best.

Louisa May Alcott curls in the softness of a threadbare settee, a book held before her face like a parlor lady's fan. *Pilgrim's Progress*. Usually an engrossing read, but today Louisa May finds herself distracted by Mr. Lane—her parents' newest guest—ever pacing, pacing, back and forth across their cottage. Floorboards creak and squall. Around him: a flurry of bodies, speculation. The Alcott family's cottage, these past few days, has been especially cacophonous. Mr. Lane, Mr. Emerson, Mr. Thoreau, Miss Foord. They gather and talk. Come and go. Dust—stirred into the air like writhing apparitions—resettles on bookshelves already raucous with desiccated butterflies, wilting daisies, cobwebs, bits of ribbon. It's this clutter that often makes Mr. Lane scowl and Miss Foord laugh and allows the stealthy Mr. Emerson to "mislay" money for her ever-needy family.

"My son," says Mr. Lane, pausing his pacing to voice a coherent thought. "The Shakers won't return him. They won't even let me see him."

To Louisa May, this news is disappointing. She does not care for Mr. Lane. He is nothing like her much-adored Mr. Thoreau: almost a child himself, appreciative of the daisies she's started leaving on his doorstep. Mr. Lane has no interest in daisies. When they lived together at Fruitlands—his family and hers—she'd come to hate his chore charts and lessons on essential virtues (Obedience, Self-denial, Industry, Silence). But, at Fruitlands, Mr. Lane's son—William—had been her playmate.

In the precious little time there'd been for playing.

"I asked and asked to see my boy. I demanded." Mr. Lane half sits, half trips, on a seesawing rocking chair. He steadies himself, rubs his hands across his cheeks, his skin as coarse as granite. Eyes as cold as coal. "But those people, they just hold up the contract. Point to my signature. 'He's indentured,' they say."

Louisa May's mother offers Mr. Lane a lumpy pear.

Louisa May's father offers up recollections of old times: the summer nights spent philosophizing and singing and sharing at Fruitlands—leaving out the lesser bits: the calloused hands and arguments, the infirmities and empty bellies. The exodus.

"What else can I do?"

Louisa May senses the heat of impending surrender: this man who once scorned her family for its bonds now aching for his only son. From behind her book, she hears a sob escape his throat like the scraping grind of a millstone.

"Remind me why you left the Shakers," says Louisa May's mother in a manner that suggests she already knows. "Your letters made their way of life sound wonderful."

Mr. Lane throws up his hands. "They aren't serious enough about establishing heaven on Earth," he says. "The Shakers claim to be spiritually informed, yet more than half elect to dine on meat!"

Louisa May wonders what has really left Mr. Lane so unsettled. His unreachable indentured son? Or that he could not enact his espoused ideals of a universal family?

"—extortionate monetary demands—"

Was it not the same at Fruitlands?

"—and their schooling, just outrageous—"

She is studying the man so closely that she fails to notice her mother come to stand beside her. A hand brushes Louisa May's hair, pats her shoulder.

"Perhaps," says Mrs. Alcott, "you could make the love argument." She glances at her husband, who has remained uncharacteristically quiet. Louisa feels the grip on her shoulder tighten, the bruising press of unwavering affection. "As I see it, you have two options. You can leave William with the Shakers and move on with your life."

Charles Lane says nothing.

"Or you can go before the Shakers and argue the preeminence of paternal love. That blood trumps all other bonds."

There is another long silence. The air in the cottage turns brittle, and Louisa feels she should not breathe for fear of breaking something.

"Would such an argument be so difficult?" Mrs. Alcott smiles grimly at Mr. Lane. "Would not such an argument be worth it?"

A boy must remember his lessons: that impartiality is more important than prosperity. Good manners eclipse intelligence. That a speck of dust might seem of little weight within the wider cosmos, just as a drop of water might be lost in the sea, but the earth is composed of dust and droplets, just as every gesture a man makes amounts to his character. From *The Future Consequences of Present Actions*, the Shaker schoolhouse guide: "A second is a short space of time, but without it there are no centuries."

Aboard the *Shenandoah*, a packet ship bound for Liverpool, the chief mate makes his evening rounds. The air is whip sharp. The sea, purple-dark and fidgeting. Most passengers have retired below for their evening meals, though a solitary figure persists on the upper deck, staring out across the water.

"Cold aren't ye?" says the chief mate, approaching. He chuckles, eyeing the man's thin linen shirt, wet with sea spray and nearly translucent. "Wouldn't want to catch yer death would ye, before we make our landing?"

The man, though visibly shivering, whirls around and sneers. "Weather," he says, with pious authority, "cannot assault the human soul."

Then he turns again to the horizon, as straight and thin as a pair of pursed lips.

A boy must think of the good days among the Shakers: the summer picnics, the nutting and the berrying, the swimming and the skating, the barn raisings and chopping frolics, the corn roasts. A boy must think of now and no other time. He must lie straight in his bed and strive to sleep in a manner that is unbroken and without dreams. If a boy has dreams, he must report them to his Caretaker. When entering the room to speak to his Caretaker, a boy must bow three times, kneel, then confess his every crooked step. Each wayward thought. He must then proceed to the meetinghouse for worship, taking care not to gaze out upon surrounding fields: grasses feathery in the dusk, or the sky, stacked with clouds like the surf of a purpling sea. He must not wonder. He must not yearn. A boy must enter the meetinghouse and form two lines with the other children. His hands must be folded with the thumb and forefinger of the right hand covering the left. He must not laugh. He must not glare. He must sing low. When the time comes to dance, a boy must not scuff his feet. He must step with the right foot first, and he must step carefully so as to avoid the shoes of those in front of him. He must not rub against the wall or drift out of line. He must feel ecstatic but not too ecstatic. He must stop when the song stops and file out into night without speaking. A boy must complete his evening chores before dark. He must never make a fire in a stove without supervision. There must be no wood piled near the stove nor the spit box set beneath the stove. The stove must always be shut tight before all leave the room. A boy must return to his sleeping quarters by nine. If a door is locked, a boy must not go on rattling and knocking. It is not meant to be opened.

Flowers
for
Prisoners

In San Miguel de Allende, long-necked poinsettia peer from walled patios, blossoms painted *pimentón* red.

Behind massive mahogany doors—iron studded, Spanish colonial—geraniums riot pink and peppery, frail petals blowing back into cobblestoned streets, settling in the dust, the barrios.

Yellow marigolds. Crimson gladioli. The white teeth of lime trees coming into bloom. They lance their stems through metal grates, over the cracked glass razoring wall edges, as bougainvillea—dark knuckled and rangy—cling to the turn of padlocks.

Lucia has a key.

Lucia has a key to the first gate, the heavy chain; the second gate, the metal door; the third gate, the house door.

She opens them all. The house is quiet. Always, in moments like this, she wonders if the owner is dead.

She has come across them dead before. *Muertos.* Tucked in bed, still as stone, or broken at the bottom of the stairs. Or sometimes she finds them halfway gone. Calling for help from the shower, pink and puckered and like newborn mice, eyes fearful.

Mostly, though, they are alive and waiting for her. The retirees. The snowbirds. *Los norteamericanos.* Gringos. They mention the spilled coffee grounds in the kitchen. The cat hair and the linens. Sometimes, they try the scraps of Spanish that stick in their fading minds. *Haaasta looaygo! Aaadeeos!* They are always going places: to book club, salsa class, theater showings, shuffleboard, tea. They come to San Miguel for the climate, for the "culture," they call it. They are usually nice.

Ms. Vivian is not home. Her cat yawns, arches its back, rubs its tail against Lucia's leg. The cat's food bowl is empty, the water too. There are no pesos piled on the kitchen counter. Ms. Vivian must have forgotten. She sometimes does. She must be out.

There is nothing that should make Lucia worried, and yet she feels pins in her belly—the prick of impending calamity—or perhaps they are always there these days, those pins.

Lucia cleans the bathroom first, then the living room, the bedroom, the kitchen.

She locks the doors behind her.

San Miguel—a colonial city, licked with color—on the side of a hill once rich with silver, dazzling the conquistadors, and later, the revolutionaries, the GIs, and the poets. Liquor, running through the gutters. Prayers in the air. La Parroquia at the top of the city like a proud nesting bird—feathered pink—and chiming all hours of the day.

Lucia finds Hugo at home.

Did you hear? He is covered in dust, is sweat-soaked. His grin makes Lucia nearly drop her grocery bags: the tortillas and chicken, the Coca-Cola.

For three weeks she has waited for news of her brother, Arturo, waited to hear—

Hugo motions toward their television set, the leap and lunge of football players, an airborne embrace.

Lucia's heart sinks. This is not the news she wanted: news of a phone call from the States. The words *Soy vivo. I am alive.*

Giving the TV a little nod, Lucia brings her basket to the kitchen. She should know that Hugo will not likely speak of Arturo anytime soon. That boy. Her half-brother really, a decade younger than she, they'd raised him like a son. That's what Hugo used to call him. *Mi hijo.*

Now Hugo won't even say her brother's name.

Lucia fries chicken tortillas, cooks squash blossom soup. She and Hugo drink the Coca-Cola. Through their walls they hear the neighbors' TVs all tuned to the same channel: football in every house.

Hugo is in his finest mood. He squeezes her backside, kisses her cheek. Like her, he has a broad face, nut-brown skin, a growing paunch. Unlike her, he was born outside San Miguel. Once he'd farmed in Oaxaca, but now he makes more money selling hats to tourists. Straw hats, stacked thirty high on his head as he circles the square outside La Parroquia. The sun, he likes to say, it used to bring me corn. Now it brings me gringo sunburns.

Shouldn't we have heard from Arturo by now? Lucia cannot help asking.

Hugo's face darkens. His chewing slows. He does not speak, but Lucia hears his answer anyway: It's Arturo's own fault if he's dead in the Chihuahuan, vultures circling. After all we've done.

Lucia's husband, he is not a cruel man. But he is also not a man who finds his own feelings easy to face.

Does she dare look at hers?

Lucia clears away their dishes. A neighbor stops by for a smoke. Then her cousins, Francis and Francesca, for gossip. Outside, evening soaks the streets, jasmine in the air. The roof dogs howl. In this part of town, doorways glow open and warm.

The cartel? The cartel. It seemed so much a part of Mexico, you couldn't tell the two apart. Who was kidnapping, embezzling, killing? *La Policía o los Narcos?* Along the highways, you pass pickup trucks carrying men, machine guns; you pass the graves.

Sinaloa. La Familia. Tijuana. Los Zetas. Gulf. Beltrán Leyva. Juárez.

San Miguel is safe, though. It's where the cartel's grandmothers live—or that's what people say, half joking, half not. It's where the gringos go.

Lucia returns to Ms. Vivian's two days later. Sunflowers bob on the patio, black-eyed and fringed in yellow. Inside, the house is spotless. The cat follows Lucia around, mewing as if to apologize. Lucia looks for a note. She is sure she would have seen one the first time, but she looks anyway: opening draws, lifting woven rugs, fluttering the pages of books. What would Ms. Vivian think if she suddenly returned? That Lucia was snooping. Stealing? There would be a fuss, no doubt. Ms. Vivian's pink mouth crinkling tight. Her grey curls coiled as if preparing to spring. A fuss, but then the two of them would find an understanding. They'd laugh. Lucia liked the old woman, despite herself.

There is no note. Lucia begins cleaning the house, though it does not need to be cleaned again. She wipes down the mahogany frames from Oxal. Mosaics from Dolores Hidalgo. The papier-mâché chicken from San Miguel's own market. Then there are the American things. The photograph of two pale daughters. The silver watch. A bureau full of sweaters and beige slacks. A box of Cheerios.

Lucia picks up the watch, lays the cool metal across her wrist.

Is this what her brother wanted?

Arturo. He was seventeen, thick without being fat. Serious, even as a little boy. He had a handsome face, she'd always believed, though Arturo had never seemed interested in chasing girls. Never much interested in school either, though his grades were fine. A waste of time, he'd said. He'd wanted something else.

What else? What else? What else?

You could get you a job here, she'd told him. Hugo could arrange it.

For the gringos? The old farts? Arturo had grimaced. He looked north, as if he could see Texas from their window.

You would work for the gringos there too, Lucia had said.

Arturo shook his head. No, it will be different.

Maybe Lucia had told herself, it would be different. Maybe Arturo would find a better life. Up there. Still, she had not wanted to see her family splinter, separated by so much distance, so she told Hugo of Arturo's plans, hoping her husband would convince her brother otherwise.

Instead Hugo answered: Let him go if he thinks he's so tough.

What had Lucia said? Nothing. She'd been afraid to upset either man.

He should go—Hugo's words—if that's what he thinks it means to be brave.

And Arturo had gone.

Of course it hurt her. It hurt them both, though Hugo hid his grief with anger. But at whom was he angry, really? At himself for having never tried the crossing? For being afraid? For spending his days circling La Parroquia, selling stacked hats and posing for tourist photos?

She herself had never considered leaving. She had too many roots dug deep in San Miguel. There were her sisters and cousins and friends. Her life was ground into the stones of this place, bubbling up in the Izcuinapan springs.

People did leave, though. They left all the time. The more gringos in San Miguel, the higher the price of gasoline, of meat. Most locals lived on the outskirts now, walking to town for work or Mass. They all wonder how much farther they'll be pushed before the walk becomes too far.

But going north? There were so many dangers. The trigger-happy border patrol. Rattlesnakes. Death of thirst. Corrupt *coyotes*. The cartel.

The cartel.

Lucia pauses polishing Ms. Vivian's ceramic vases. She had nearly forgotten the old woman, her employer's unexplained absence. What if Ms. Vivian had taken a trip—to Michoacán maybe—hadn't she mentioned wanting to see the *yácatas*? Was it so impossible that she could have been kidnapped? On one hand, the gringos triple-locked their houses, but in Mexico they also turned a little wild. Wild enough to move here. What was it they wanted? To make their lives a little richer before they left this world? The local doctor knew. He'd told Lucia, shaking his head as he whispered, gonorrhea. Septuagenarians, octogenarians: they aren't careful at that age. What do they have to lose? Lucia remembers Ms. Vivian talking about how dating could be difficult, because men her age were scarce. *Todos mueren primero.* They all die first.

The old woman always spoke in the present when muddling through Spanish. Most gringos did. It was the only way they knew the language.

And Arturo? He'd always used the future: *Voy a ser grande.* I will be great.

The thought makes Lucia drop her dusting rag, steady herself against a shelf of cornhusk dolls. Each figurine in a dress—hand-painted turquoise, magenta, emerald green—and tied with ribbons. Each face forever blank. The dolls, their quietness, make Lucia want to scream. She wants to tear these tiny women limb by limb. She wants them gone from sight.

She grabs one, her fist around its torso. The husk-doll is light. Air, mostly.

Lucia hesitates, then begins to squeeze. This doll, so like the kind her grandmother once made from the leftovers of tamales, probably cost more than a week's wages.

Lucia stares into the blank face. She wills the doll to speak. She wills it to admit that it does not belong on this shelf—that it does not even belong in this house—that it belongs, instead, in the hands of a little girl: a girl playing in a straw-strewn alley, making castles from empty crates, feather beds from the molting blossoms of purple jacaranda trees.

The doll stays quiet.

Swiftly, before Lucia can stop herself, she tucks the doll into the folds of her skirt.

Of all things to steal, why this?

Lucia cannot answer her own question. She moves instead to the door. She knows she should tell someone about Ms. Vivian's absence—she should report it to the woman's neighbors, the police—but what if the absence means nothing? Suppose Ms. Vivian had told Lucia she was leaving and Lucia had forgotten, her mind distracted by Arturo. It wouldn't be Lucia's first mistake.

But that cat, left alone?

Lucia has another house to clean—there are wages to earn, bills to pay—and yet she cannot bring herself to go. The day is getting hot, shadows melting into tiled eaves. San Miguel's streets stutter full with green taxicabs, pickup trucks loaded with chicken crates. An unhappy donkey pulls an ice cream cart. Lucia leaves Ms. Vivian's house and hurries along the sloping sidewalks—past the outdoor restaurants, umbrellas blooming, gringo patrons dazed on mezcal—all the while the corn husk doll hides inside her skirt. A garbage boy runs alongside her ringing his cowbell and calling for trash. She sees her cousins, Francis and Francesca. They wave to her, but she ducks into the market alley around raw slabs of meat through the sizzle of grills and mesquite smoke. She hurries past La Parroquia—its rosy towers, chiming bells—careful also to avoid Hugo, who is here somewhere, selling hats. She hurries until she reaches a smaller church, braced against a wall. Oratorio de San Felipe Neri. Its vast wooden doors cracked open. She slides in, grateful for the cool interior. All around: a dim gold light filtering in from skylights, oil paintings depicting a saint's painful ordeal. At this time of day, it is nearly empty.

Lucia finds a seat and closes her eyes. She thinks of all the people she knows going north, while the gringos go south. Bodies in a two-way flood. A confused river. It's strange, really. Both groups seem to be looking for the same thing.

Lucia tries to pray, to ask for protection for her brother and Ms. Vivian. For mercy. She feels she should ask for mercy for herself also, but for what she isn't sure. The stolen doll? Not that, no. She does not feel sorry. She does not feel anything; her mind is drained of words. She can only see, and she sees the worst possibilities: Arturo on his knees, his mouth tied, face swollen. He'd never agree to be a drug mule. She sees Ms. Vivian too, that frail woman, white skin scorched, earlobes leaking blood where her earrings were ripped out. Lucia knows what is done, even to old women. To boys.

Lucia sees the dark nostrils of a double barrel rifle. Her breath quickens. Is it impossible, yet possible, that these two might be together? Given what they'd wanted—*what else? what else? what else?*—something different, something better than they had. She pictures the pair kneeling, side-by-side, on a sunbaked patch of desert earth.

She waits for pain but feels instead the husk-doll nestled at her side. A body light as air, heavy as memory.

Out beyond, in that desert, stumpy cacti are beginning to blossom. Red flares clustered among spiring thorns. Petaled crowns of naked white. Everything opening, opening now, under a sky unflinching and blue.

Acid

You'll say it was because your parents didn't understand you—that's why you left—but really it's because they
understood you too well. They looked at you, their daughter, the
way they read labels in the grocery store. All the ingredients adding up. They watched you with faint, serious joy playing across
their faces.

"Sally Sunshine," people call you now: the other hippies and run-
aways and spirit seekers. "Sally Sunny Sunshine," they say, because you hardly ever stay inside. You sit in the sun until your
fair skin burns, the heat branding your shoulders, your cheeks—
your nipples when you go topless—burning until the skin blisters

and peels. The skin: it lifts off the surface of your arms like a pale thin rust.

"Sally, Sally Sunshine," the others sing. "What are you going to do today?"

How good it feels to be misunderstood, to be looked at as something unknowable. You do things to keep them guessing. You do things to keep yourself guessing.

"You're so young," says one of the men. Another sour-smelling, matted-haired man. You grab his crotch and look him straight in the eyes and laugh.

The house belongs to an old artist. He has a long beard and skin like a raisin, and sometimes he disappears into the desert, then comes back and makes tea and sits on the porch, still staring into the desert.

You aren't sure he even realizes everyone else is there.

You are a queen. Your hair is loose and ropey. Your skin burned. You wear a long dress and let it drag behind you. You walk barefoot everywhere. You step on burrs, in coyote shit, on nails. You don't care. That is part of your mystery: how little you care. You are an animal. You burrow into pillows. You speak only in howls. You are a pure thing; you do what you want. You do not help clean. You do not help cook. You won't say sorry.

Sometimes the others talk about ideals: freedom, equality, peace. You like the sound of the words. You like that you can put the words in your pocket, let them jangle alongside raven feathers, an old penny, a bullet casing. Things that seem both precious and worthless.

"Categorical," says the old man, the artist, rocking on the porch. He looks out at the desert. He looks and looks and looks.

There are the mountains, naked. Scrubbed to brown. Everything naked, too hot for anything else.

And the smoke, the sweat smells, the candle burning; bare feet, ringing bells

Even now it's in your brain. Your parents' words, like acid, worming inside you. "Sally," they used to say, "our brave little girl. Our smart little girl. You're going to do big things. You're going to do important things." And how it pains you, remembering this, how it makes you writhe and dance and press your fingers into the sharp ends of saguaro spines, thinking, knowing, that they still might be right.

Ephemera

It's Tuesday; Vera hits another cowboy town. She wears each day in a stratum of skin salt and red desert dust—the only stuff that sticks. Two weeks ago she found the hole in her pack, noticed her belongings leaking like prizes from a battered piñata. Last time she checked, she only had eight sticks of chewing gum, five Band-Aids, three disguises, two blankets, and a dried out scorpion. The four hundred and twenty-three dollars—delicately lifted from Dale's stash—now mark a trail down Interstate 8 back to Tucson.

Easy come, easy go, she tells herself, ducking through the jingle-ingle of another diner door, inhaling greasy-griddled steam.

But it's not easy and she knows it. When mornings yawn above her campsites, pinked and innocent, Vera gets a gut punch of guilt. She's been missing Aimee Lee since April. It's the only thing she feels—besides hungry now and then—and when Vera gets hungry, she finds a twenty-four hour diner and a lonely man. The men remind her of her boyfriend Dale—sluggish and immobile—but an empty stomach never got no one nowhere. Vera's got her little girl to find.

"Well now," a voice cajoles, its owner stationed on a stool. "What's a pretty young thing like you doing here?"

Vera sets her pack on a black square of the checkerboard floor. She dredges up a smile, flicks her hair. It's a dirty blonde in sunshine—red and green in the neon blaze of *Open Late, Live Music, Coors*—but under the fluorescents, it's delicate and pearled. She feels the man's gaze run loose over her ringless fingers, slide down the hips she's sewn up in overalls. They are deep set, his eyes, and dark as oil wells. His jacket says *O'Reilly* in yellow embroidery.

He buys her scrambled eggs and sausage links.

"Mind if I ask something?" says Vera, after wolfing down her food. She leans into the sooty breath of her breakfast sponsor, smiling sweet-as-apple-pie. This man is hoping to show her the inside of his truck: to press her face against its vinyl seats as if that's all she ever wanted to see. "Tell me," she says, taking a final swig of coffee, swishing the bitterness around her mouth, "what's an ugly old thing like you doing here?"

The diner door clangs closed on the answers—its jingle-ingle laughing—and Vera squints into sunshine: a town called Hellswell. "Home of the Copper Camp Mine," reads a sign, paint scabbed and peeling. The place is ghosted, stupefied by heat.

Vera has run out of missing person flyers to post, so she finds a bulletin board, flips over a gun show poster, and scrawls out a description of Aimee Lee. *Six Years Old—Brown Eyes—A Loose Tooth—Likes Bubbles and Horses.* She writes Dale's phone number at the bottom. It's the only one she can think of besides the police, and they can't do anything now. They'd told her that themselves. Stooped inside Dale's trailer and taken off their hats; tugged them on when they left.

Ain't that something, thinks Vera, fanning her face with her own hat: a wide-brim straw number, smelling faintly of the maple syrup pooled on diner counters. She's hungry again, but there's so much ground to cover, a whole planet of red gritty ground.

Ain't that something, walking in and out of someone else's life?

Carlos "Cosmos" Rockingham Pete knows a thing or two about women. He knows their mouths make red O's when putting on lipstick. He knows they carry secrets like spare change. He knows enough that when he sees a grimy blonde teetering toward Cosmos' Treasure & Trash—the junk shop that doubles as his home—that she'll be staying the night.

It won't be in his bed, though. Hot damnation.

"I got a room," he declares, before she's even at his door. She nods and he reckons they already get along. They both know talking isn't the only way of speaking. Carlos Pete is a spiritual man, though he'd never admit it. He's always been sure that when fate pulls strings, it ain't wise to pull back. You gotta take what comes same as you gotta give what's taken away.

"First door on the left," he tells her, pointing up the stairs. "Shake out the blankets in case critters got in."

It's just that normally Carlos Pete gives drifters a bit of bread and directions to the train yard.

Was this a sign of mental decline, him welcoming strangers? His store hasn't pulled a profit in four months. In fact, there hasn't been a customer all day. What's more, he already has a lodger, taken in last week: a soft-spoken, shiny-eyed Californian who called himself "Smythson." At least that kid had made a pledge to do some chores.

This woman, though.

"You want a drink?" he hollers in the direction of her room.

She answers with the box-spring creak of a body on a mattress.

I'm a damn fool, he thinks to himself, *a fat old sucker.*

The woman had been looking over her shoulder like she had the devil behind her. Maybe she did, for all he knows. What devil wouldn't want to chase a thing like her? Blue-eyed, with bare shoulders budding from her overall straps. A pair of *Playboy* tits. And it's been so long since Carlos Pete had something pretty to look at—even if her pretty is buried beneath an inch of grit—even if he's likely three times her age. He certainly can't look at himself. Paunched belly, skid-marked skin, ponytail gone gray: mirrors show his house another stranger.

He hauls himself up to her room and peers inside. She's fallen asleep with her boots still on. It's not yet six o'clock.

Musta been damn tired, thinks Carlos Pete. He rubs his own neck, stiff with a tiredness you can't sleep off.

When Vera dreams, she dreams of Aimee Lee as a silky-winged bird. She imagines herself back at Dale's, her daughter overhead; her daughter circling the white grid of mobile homes, too joyful to drop down.

Vera last saw her daughter at the Mission Hill playground. Her daughter, flitting in and out of the jungle gym like a wild bird. A giddy green hummer. A grinning goldfinch. A trogon, blood-bellied and singing. Vera had sat watching on a park bench, resting from her shift at the auto parts warehouse. A dizzy kind of work. An echoing reshuffle that cracked her hands and frayed her mind. She'd closed her eyes for a moment—at least, it felt like a moment—and pictured Aimee Lee soaring into the air, finding wings.

When she opened them, her daughter was gone.

At first, Vera thought Aimee Lee really had flown off. She'd been happy in that instant, peaceful even—believing her daughter had escaped to something better—believing at least her little girl was free.

Carlos Pete stays up all night, thinking the kinds of thoughts he hasn't in years. Big thoughts. Terrible thoughts. Heavy-footed thoughts that stomp across his mind. There's a woman sleeping in the house, first time in years. She's a live wire. A tripped switch. Carlos Pete feels walls rise around him, blood bolt through his veins.

"Smythson," he calls, and his boy-guest emerges grinning from the cellar, cheeks dirt-smudged, spark plug in hand. The kid is seventeen—a runaway, no doubt—just as Carlos Pete had once been. Not that the kid knows. The kid doesn't know much about anything, besides the wiry entrails of electronics. Carlos Pete has kept quiet out of habit. But all of a sudden he feels his words shake loose, he sees them tumble into sight.

Way back, before the years piled up, Carlos Pete was one heck of a lady lover. He was a Casanova, a virtuoso, a phenomenon. He had cheekbones like flying buttresses and strong arms that swung the pretty girls of Hellswell round in circles. His mamma cited an ancestry threading through the Anasazi, winding among Spanish Conquistadors, wayward Franciscans, homeless homesteaders, and a whole contingent of bright-eyed prospectors. His blood was a cocktail of passion; women got drunk just looking in his eyes. Was it really such a surprise, with blood like that, when his feet got itchy? He split town for a post in the Navy at age twenty-three. He left his mamma's house and all the pretty girls weeping behind.

It was in the sea, in the warm sweep of the Kuroshio Current, the spray shivering up off a storm surge, that Carlos Pete found his heart's match. The ocean left him love-struck in a way no woman ever had—not that he didn't meet more women as well— he met flamenco dancers, yam pickers, Danish princesses, spice merchantesses, actresses disguised as men. He never said no to any of them, but he never quite said yes either, even after quitting the service somewhere near Singapore. The water always lured him back.

For his mamma, Carlos Pete mailed home the glittering oddities of the world. Boxes full of ostrich feathers. Teacups carved from narwhal horns. Pressed hibiscus from Hawaii. Once, he sent a chip off a Greenland glacier, cut to sparkle like a huge diamond. She'd open an empty crate, he knew, save for one damp breath of the borealis: spectral and sublime. The gifts were the best kind of restitution he could manage for his absence.

All told, for twenty years Carlos Pete washed up on palmed shorelines and into thronged seaports, then later left on the tides. He spun round in cyclones, drifted through the dark net of latitudes, longitudes, and never got caught.

Then one day a letter found him, pronouncing his mamma dead.

Carlos Pete arrived at his boyhood home with plans to sell the place quick. As sole inheritor, he figured he'd spend his earnings on a sailboat. There seemed no reason to stick around. All the pretty girls he'd known in Hellswell weren't girls anymore. They weren't so pretty either.

But the house wouldn't sell. It watched the highway like an old dog, from sunup to sundown, too whipped to move. A curious property, sure—Carlos Pete's grandfather built it from the tornadofied remnants of an old mining town—but not the kind of place most people want to start a life. And it sure as heck wasn't where Carlos Pete wanted to finish his.

Trouble was, even if he had the funds, the house was gorged with belongings, generations of them. Cupboards swelled with pick axes, cake pans, a lifetime subscription to *Reader's Digest*. And everything Carlos Pete ever mailed to his mother—every jeweled teapot or furred Russian hat—sulked throughout the house like a writ of habeas corpus.

Well dang, thinks Smythson, when his host's words run dry. *Aren't I lucky to be lodging with such an adventuresome man?*

He is seventeen and has just grown into his ears.

Vera wakes up with a face full of lace. Her pillow is soft, soaked in soap-smells, a whiff of tobacco. She lurches to her feet, sets the floorboards groaning: they've already guessed she's sneaking away. Vera doesn't care. It was an accident—a fever dream—her coming to this house. She's got to get back on the road, to keep looking for Aimee Lee.

Then, a glittery wink. A jewelry box on a bureau. Vera creaks toward it, upends the lid, fumbles for gemstone facets, the milky orbs of pearls: a goodbye gift before she leaves.

"Awake at last," calls a voice from the doorway.

Vera jumps, her cheeks going hot. "Who is it?" she growls, fiercer than she feels.

A light bursts on and Vera sees an old man. She's unexpectedly pleased. He's got a ponytail like a long gray tassel, a face mapped with wrinkles. "Welcome to Cosmos' Treasures and Trash," he says, tilting into a bow. "Open for business and at your service."

Vera eyes the door—an escape route to Aimee Lee—but the scent of frying onions has crept up the stairs. She trails the old man to his kitchen. She can call him Carlos Pete, he says. She can have herself a seat. Vera watches liquid egg yolks slip into a bowl like sinking suns. She stares at their sizzle as Carlos Pete explains how he turned his house into a store. Woohee, he tells her, she should've seen the first customers: a pair of tourists buttered up with sunscreen. Asked for directions and ended up buying a painting of a Navajo chief off his living room wall.

"Just like that?" asks Vera, still not sure if the omelet is for her.

"Just like that," says Carlos Pete. "Twenty years I been trying to sell this house, but it turns out people would rather buy what's inside it. So sales keep my electricity flowing, my belly full."

Vera's own belly kicks and screams. Again, she looks at the door.

"There ya go," says Carlos Pete. He sets a steaming plate before her.

Vera lifts her fork, a price tag dangling: "25¢."

Carlos Pete continues, "Yup, we've got pretty much everything here: vases, vacuum cleaners, jelly jars, postage stamps, model trains, earrings, ottomans, paint brushes, snow globes, Barbie dolls, chain saws, tomahawks, Italian Lira—why we've even got teenage boys—" he motions toward a tall youth stumbling sleepy-eyed into the kitchen. The boy goes rigid when he sees her, as if he's been electrocuted.

Vera ignores him, stabs her omelet. Aimee Lee would've loved this place, she thinks—the old man too—the grandfather she never got.

She'll leave tomorrow, she decides. One day holed up won't make a difference.

"You know ma'am," murmurs Carlos Pete, as if he's already read her mind, "Smythson here has got my shower fixed."

It's a story that's been chewed up and spit out a thousand times over, but that can't change the fact of the matter: Smythson fell in love at first sight. Laying eyes on Vera was like reeling in the kickback of a .45 Magnum. It was a face full of gunpowder. A ricocheting mind. While Smythson was unsure of plenty—the existence of God, the mechanics of sex—he knew such things were dangerous. Loving and gun-shooting, their dangers never kept people from messing around with them. He knew that too.

In another life—his former life—Smythson might have wrung out the moment in a leather-bound journal. *I met a woman,* he'd have written in loopy cursive letters, *her lips as red as a coyote's post-kill.* But he'd given up journaling. He'd given it up the same night he took his first sputtering sip of Carlos Pete's whiskey, held his first gun, took his first wild shot at a stack of cans in the man's backyard—his first night as a runaway—the first night anything worth recording had ever happened to him.

And besides, there wasn't a journal big enough for all his thoughts on Vera.

Running away had been easy enough for Smythson. He told his folks he'd been accepted to a summer seminar for future engineers. A rural retreat in Nevada. He'd be out of touch. As his bus wheezed from the Newport station, he'd waved goodbye to the tops of their heads—his father's comb-over, his mother's silk scarf—as if farewelling his own future. It stood on the sidewalk and waved back. The college degree and tennis club membership. The checkbook and heavy ballpoint pen. The obituary.

His getaway bus shot east out of Orange County until familiar neighborhoods shriveled up and disappeared. After a route change in San Bernardino, even jaded storefronts slunk away. Smythson pressed his face against the windowpane. The sight of the Sonora set his fingertips tingling; he longed for something, though he wasn't sure what.

Then he met Vera and gave it a name.

Vera stays a second night and then the night after, until—three weeks deep—Carlos Pete can count on her creaking down the stairs each morning. She's had plenty of troubles, he learns. A child stolen some four months back. A threadbare relationship. No family. They were real troubles too, not like the tales he squeezed out of Smythson: stories as long and snaky as the Colorado.

"I should get moving, shouldn't I?" she says each morning. "Keep looking?"

Carlos Pete doesn't know all the details of her missing girl, but he expects they aren't optimistic. He imagines she feels the same way he does about his house—his pretending that it might someday sell. It's a dull sickness, hope, one they both can't bear to cure.

"No reason to rush," he tells her, same as he tells himself.

So she stays. And, sooner than seems reasonable, it's as though all three have always lived together. Most evenings they play gin rummy at the kitchen table. Or they sit on the back porch watching cars snarl down the highway, Smythson smoking spiced tobacco despite his frequent coughing fits.

Carlos Pete had always considered himself a soloist. Even in his early days—in the Navy's orchestratic frenzy, in a woman's euphony of moans—but now, anchored by possessions, he finds himself savoring company that won't quit. His guests lighten the crush of unsold objects. Their stay may dry up the last of his dough, but he decides he doesn't care.

When no one's watching Vera sneaks phone calls.

"Hullo?" says her boyfriend Dale, his voice stretched thin and full of holes. "Vera, that you?"

Vera holds the receiver against her ear, not saying a word. She never does. She likes hearing the swell of Dale's panic, his *now listen*'s like gasps of air. He'd gotten angry when she first called, hollering, "You get your butt back here, Vera James. I mean it." Now, though, his voice has lost its edge. He tells her that Aimee Lee's gone, that Vera's gotta quit denying; that their daughter's never coming back.

Then why should I? Vera nearly says it out loud. She grinds the phone back into place, wishing she'd be comforted by someone else's loss.

To Carlos Pete's surprise, when customers pull up to his house on dirt-sputtering Harleys or wing-backed Cadillacs or busted-out minivans, they begin buying a bit more than usual. It's thanks to Smythson's repair work, Carlos Pete suspects. Or Vera's incidental luminescence. Having found a pair of white gloves and a flowered frock in the attic, she floats around the house like a time-traveled movie star, lending every tarnished Winchester or frayed quilt a little more mystique.

Carlos Pete reminds himself not to get his hopes too high. The increase in sales could be a blip, an anomaly, the result of a meteor convention just down the road. Nothing to throw a party over, surely. And yet Carlos Pete feels more vigorous than he has in years.

"You ma'am," he tells Vera one afternoon, cheered by the sale of a taxidermied armadillo, "are something pretty special. You know that?"

Usually, Vera ducks from his compliments. She'll raise a question like a bulwark, say, "What if I don't, Mr. Carlos Pete?" Or more evasively, "Who's afraid of the big bad wolf?" She's a hurting woman—he knows that and doesn't blame her—but today Carlos Pete notices a prickly pear blossom pinned to her dress like a corsage, its crimson color seeping up into her cheeks. A blush. He's certain of it.

Carlos Pete tells Vera he's got something she ought to hear. He edges to a record player, puts on a syrupy chant, and takes her hand.

"I got this from a gypsy in Cameroon," he says, leading her through some steps. The stiffness in his limbs doesn't recede, but she flows around him easily, like water. Smythson appears in the living room door, watching.

Carlos Pete never mentions it, but at times he imagines the three of them as family. He wonders if he could've married a woman like Vera, so feral she might understand him. He wonders if they could've made a life together. Had a son like Smythson: solemn, industrious.

"Son," he'd tell the boy, "all women love to dance. That's the truest thing there is."

But Carlos Pete can't say it. The words would loose a termite's appetite, burrow deep into the feelings he's long since shuttered off. So instead, he lets the music weep. It floods the house with off-key warbles, melodies swirling around table legs and sinking between floorboards.

Never mind that he's too old now. Never mind that Smythson watches Vera out of the corner of his eye, and Vera watches the windows. "What are you looking for?" he's asked her, even though it's not hard to tell. She's watching the birds flitting over scrubland, as if there's one she hasn't seen.

At night, Carlos Pete sleeps alone in a wrought iron bed. The same one he left when he was twenty-three.

"Come home soon," his mamma said, so many years earlier, believing he would.

He still dreams of the sea, of white sand beaches and so much water, everywhere. The kind that makes a man young again.

Vera keeps the secret because no one asks: she can't hold onto good things. They bounce off, slip away. For a moment she'd believed she'd found something different, but she should've known better. It's her fault things are selling from the house. More every day. The three of them have been eating out of frying pans, after all, ever since a stranded tour bus cleaned out the chinaware. Closets are showing their backsides.

"Get out," her father had said, when she lost the last strand of their family's reputation. "Get your whore-ass out."

She couldn't even keep hold of Aimee Lee.

She hadn't meant to overhear Carlos Pete on the phone.

"You're serious?" he'd exclaimed, delighted and dismayed. "You want to buy my house?"

Vera knows what that's like: to be filled with five shades of feeling. She's been so happy for the first time in a long time, and yet so sorry to keep Aimee Lee waiting.

"A Dairy Queen? You know this property's historic."

Vera leans against the kitchen door, closes her eyes. There's always a moment when a mind can change. She hears the ticker tape of Carlos Pete's, whirring through what he'd be getting, what he'd give up.

"Well," he says at last. "I'll be damned."

Smythson always considered himself good with questions. He'd answered them his whole life—for his parents and French teachers and the straight-backed believers of the United Church of Christ—but he can't find answers for Vera.

"Just my luck, ain't it?" she pipes one evening, her voice stained by sorrow, as the three of them play Parcheesi on the dining room floor.

"What're you talking about darling?" guffaws Carlos Pete, throwing open his palms. "You're winning!"

The old man says this louder than he should, but Smythson doesn't notice. He hasn't noticed, either, why they're playing on the floor—that an antique dealer hauled off the dining table. He's too busy wishing Vera had flung her smile at him, curved and fleeting, like the end of a whip.

"And there you go again, rolling a double."

The old man always knew how to answer, it seems to Smythson. Sometimes it felt as through Carlos Pete and Vera spoke a language he couldn't quite understand, as if they'd both been to a country he hadn't yet visited.

In his peripheral vision, pain wheels like a hawk.

For once, Carlos Pete finds his tongue gone sluggish. He'd sat on the news all week, waiting to see his sentiments change, but every day thrust forward another wave of conviction.

"We sold," he tells Smythson at last.

"What?" says the boy, slurping cereal from a pie pan. "The couch? The refrigerator?"

Carlos Pete grimaces. Vera had taken the news like she already knew. Practically already packed.

"Everything," he tells Smythson, more joy leaking into his voice than he intended. "The lot of it. Kit and caboodle. *Mi casa.* The house."

He encircles the boy in his arms so he doesn't have to look at his face.

This is not my son, he tells himself.

Even so, Carlos Pete has half a mind to say that it's the suffering that makes the good times good. That there's a dignity in striking out alone. But he can't tell lies the way he used to, not even the comforting kind.

"It's been one hell of a pleasure," he tells Smythson, but he doesn't suggest that the kid and Vera come with him. Or that the idea has even crossed his mind. It's too late, he's decided. He's an old man now. Best grab what he's got and run.

Aimee Lee: the name howls in Vera's ears. How could she have kept herself from hearing it? How could she have forgotten?

She won't wait around for answers. It's a relief, in fact, being told to leave something so good, something better than she ever had before. It's choices that will get a girl in trouble.

"Forgive me?" she whispers. "Can you forgive me my sweet little girl?"

It takes all of two days for Cosmos' Treasures & Trash to be picked apart and shipped away by an army of antique dealers and investors and curious folks who have heard about the sale. Then, just like that, Smythson is standing roadside with his pack. He's watching Carlos Pete disappear due east on the roar of a '77 Yamaha.

He'd be flooded full of melancholy, but Vera's standing right beside him.

"I'm coming with you," he tells her, bold in the headiness of change.

Vera thrusts her thumb into the highway's sightline. She's never treated him like an adult and doesn't seem about to start. His mind churns through ways of declaring that he loves her, but then an 18-wheeler grinds to a halt and Vera climbs in. All Smythson can do is climb in after.

"Where you headed?" says the driver, a big woman with hands like boulders.

Smythson looks at Vera.

"Gawd," says the driver, "two deaf hitchhikers, what are the odds?"

At last Vera sighs, "You going toward someplace else?" which gets the driver cackling, and the brakes hissing loose, and Smythson's heart nearly drumming over the engine.

They roll east, into the domino spill of Phoenix strip malls, then hitch another ride up Highway 17, huddling under the San Francisco Peaks before skirting Indian country further on. It takes a few days before Smythson wonders whether Vera's trying to lose him, especially when she uses diner restrooms, then walks out the back door. He always pays and catches up. *Don't worry,* he tells her, *you haven't lost me.* He wishes he knew how Carlos Pete coaxed out Vera's smile, even took her by the hand. All he can manage is to stumble in her footsteps.

Not that Vera notices. After stomping through a copy shop, she starts tacking up flyers everywhere she goes. They're for her daughter, Aimee Lee. *Just Turned Seven,* they usually say, *Likes Bubbles and Horses, Maybe Other Things by Now.* The flyers go on telephone poles. They go inside town halls and mailboxes. Under napkin holders. Even to Smythson, the placement seems erratic. But instead of mentioning it, he says, "You see the size of that guy's hat?" or, "Dang, I could really use some lemonade." His words evaporate around her, but he talks anyway. He tells her about growing up in a house where everything matched: the curtains and the countertops, all a soapy powder blue. He describes mind-numbing piano lessons, fat aunts and uncles, interminable luncheons of crab cakes and watercress. He hopes she understands that, in a circulatory way, he's explaining why he loves her.

Then one afternoon—as Vera clips a flyer to a string of barbed wire—Smythson can't help blurting, "You really think that'll work?"

The words make Vera whirl around. For a moment her hot breath hits his, still sweet with pancakes eaten earlier that day. Then she slaps him hard across the face.

"Don't you dare ask that," she says. "Don't you ever ask it again, you hear?"

It's the shock that contains Smythson's tears. He's never been hit before, especially not by someone he loves. Vera turns and starts marching again. There is a long stretch of quiet—a whole mile of it maybe—with only the drag of their boots against gravel. They pass the black lick of a truck tire, icy crystals of broken glass.

Then Smythson tells her he loves her. Swiftly, sincerely, he tells her that he always has.

When Vera turns this time, she goes slow. She clamps a hand on each of his shoulders, reminding him momentarily of a high school dance.

"Smythson," she says, "aren't I old enough to be your mother?"

The gravity in her voice strikes him as tender and cruel at the same time. It makes him love her even more.

Vera swats at a mosquito trying to land on her arm. She is dreaming. She finds herself wanting to go to sleep again, inside her dream, but the mosquito keeps buzzing.

". . . and then I'll get my trust fund." The words, Smythson's, echo and expand. "We'll start a new life, you and me. I'll take care of you."

Vera finds this hard to believe—the being taken care of, not the money—but then she recalls the hour before sleep. She remembers Smythson stoking a campfire of loose railroad ties; Smythson fixing her tent and helping her inside; Smythson laying down beside her. He'd kept talking and talking as if she needed his words to go on breathing.

It must mean something: him being the first thing she can't seem to lose.

"My parents might not understand," Smythson buzzes, "but they live inside rules the way people live in castles, as if everything outside is either dangerous or unimportant."

But that means you can go back to a castle. Vera finds she suddenly wants to speak. She thinks of Smythson's folks, who must be missing him the way she misses Aimee Lee. It won't make the world anymore straight, any more balanced, with more people feeling that way.

"We need each other," says Smythson—or was that Dale's voice—was that Dale, on the phone yesterday, saying, "We need each other to get through all this."

Vera shivers. She'll never find her daughter. She's known this longer than she wants to admit. Her little girl is gone. That day at the playground: her girl had wandered off, yes, while Vera dozed on the bench. But she hadn't been stolen. She hadn't flown into the sky. She had wandered into the road and been struck by an oncoming car.

Smythson's parents, though, they could still get back their son.

In her dream, Vera lets the mosquito land on her arm; she lets the insect draw itself jewellike with blood.

The next morning, Smythson buys bus tickets. Vera makes a phone call—a long one this time—she has to ask for extra change. Then they sit on a curb in the square shade of a dumpster. The bus won't come for a few more hours.

The tickets are to Newport. They'll go there, "just briefly," Smythson tells Vera, to get his "finances in order." The promise feels good on his tongue. Vera doesn't say much about the plan, just, "Newport's where your folks live?" But Smythson isn't about to forget the night before—the way they'd held each other—the way she'd fallen asleep in his arms. He imagines the life ahead of them: fingers entwined in front of Niagara Falls, the two of them strolling among gardens on the National Mall. Maybe they'd even track down Carlos Pete bobbing offshore in a sailboat. Hear the old man's whistle of surprise.

"I'll be damned," Carlos Pete would say, thumping Smythson on the back. "You lucky bastard."

They could live together on the boat, just like they'd lived in the house. Vera would take naps below deck, rocked to sleep by the waves, while he and Carlos Pete looked out at the water.

"This kind of life," the old man might say, "it's not something you choose."

Glasses would clink, eyes would squint into sunsets, and—

Smythson's thoughts are interrupted by a red pickup pulling along the curb.

Vera stands and grabs her pack.

"What are you doing?" Smythson scrambles to his own feet, the bus tickets clenched in one fist like a paper bouquet. "Vera?" His voice cracks as she heaves her pack into the truck.

"I'm leaving," she says, lips taut and matter-of-fact, "with Dale here."

And then Smythson feels it: the sky, turquoise blue, sinking like a soaked quilt across his shoulders. He staggers under the weight. His senses smudge—the garbage smell going too bright, the parking lot tilting toward nausea. Vera opens the truck door, climbs inside, and Smythson realizes, with near amusement, that he is feeling pain. The engine revs. It is worse than anything he could have ever imagined. And yet, this—this is what he'd really wanted all along. He'd wanted to feel something. To feel alive. But how was he supposed to stand it?

How was anyone?

Smythson doesn't try to stop Vera. Even after the pickup truck has rattled away, he stays standing, tickets drooped in his hand. He's still waiting there when the bus pulls in, when its doors sigh open, ready to return him to his coin collection and science fair projects and neatly folded dress shirts. Ready to take at least one lost child home.

Delight®

We moved to Delight® when Mom ran away with a lesbian kombucha mogul. Dad said it was because his allergies bothered him in Alaska, but even my siblings and I—at the tender ages of seven, nine, nine, twelve, and thirteen—could tell he was looking for some stability. He found it in three square miles of front porches and American flags: in a place that smelled like freshly mowed lawns and—though we didn't identify the scent until later—malted milkshakes.

"Reminds me of my childhood," said Dad, our first evening in Delight®. All of us stood on our front porch surveying the neighborhood. Across the street, kids caught fireflies in Farm-

StyleGlassJars®. A husband and wife held hands as they watered their EverbloomingPinkPassionAzaleas®. A dog fetched. Crickets cricketed.

"But Dad," said my youngest sister, "didn't you grow up in inner-city Anchorage?"

Before he could answer, a parade of aproned women appeared on our porch, each bearing a different flavor pie—Berrylicious-Crumble®, Aunty'sApplePear®, PlumCobblerKabooom!!®—along with handwritten notes welcoming us to Delight®.

Dad was over the moon. He already looked younger. My siblings and I had been concerned about his blood pressure, but now the color was back in his cheeks. For the first time in months, he was telling cheesy jokes—Q: *What happened after the explosion in the French cheese factory? A: All that was left was da Brie*—and even as we groaned, we were happy to see him happy. After the women left and we'd we stuffed ourselves with pie, we watched Dad pace around the living room so excited he forgot our bedtimes.

"This is big," he said. "You all are going to love it here."

Of course, that's when we knew things would get worse.

Our lives, though, continued along Splendidly®. Dad got a job as a postman, and we'd see him walking around the neighborhood whistling and swinging his arms, pulling treats out of his pockets for dogs that wouldn't have bitten him anyways. At school, my siblings and I studied ProperHandshakeProtocol®, PerfectPiePreparation®, and Math®. We learned how to play Reputable® musical instruments—tuba, banjo, banjo, harp, and cello—and we performed monthly gigs at Delight's® Ice-CreamJamborees®. All of us, we grew up straight and cheerful. I made the baseball team and earned a HeartwarmingCome-FromBehindChampionship®. In the presence of one brown-eyed Cheerleaderette® I felt FlutteringStomachButterflies® and GoodNaturedTrepidation®. The Cheerleaderette® and I, we later participated in TenderHandHolding® during the monthly Ice-CreamJamboree®. Then again, three years later, at a church alter decorated with EverbloomingPinkPassionAzaleas® where I also got a wedding ring and a TenderKiss®.

It was Dad, strangely enough, whose satisfaction waned.

"Gosh darn it!" he exclaimed one night, during a Festive-FamilyFeast®. "You know what really gets my goat?"

Everyone else at the table went quiet, myself included. I was twenty-two by that time and had moved with my wife into a CuteCouple'sCottage®, but I ate dinner with Dad and my siblings at least once a week, despite Dad's increasing un-Pleasantness®.

"What's this about goat?" one of my sisters replied, with ample Pleasantness®. She pushed a platter of Potatoes'N'Peas'N'Ham® in Dad's direction.

Dad cackled, loud enough that I considered closing the windows so that our neighbors wouldn't hear. He had drunk about a gallon of ExtraFoamyRootbeer®, and the stuff seemed to be going to his head. None of us had asked where he had gotten the drink—we were committed to PoliteTableTalk®—but all of us could guess. Recently, there had been reports of a lurking band of Ne'er-Do-Wells just beyond the borders of Delight®. I hadn't seen them myself, but from what I'd heard, they were highly un-Reputable® and un-Polite®.

"Father," I said, "maybe we could discuss a more TenderSpecial-Topic®?" I reached across the table for my wife. We engaged in TenderHandHolding®. "There's some news we—"

Dad interrupted. "What gets me," he said, "is that you're all so damn well behaved."

My siblings and I stared at him with GoodNaturedConfusion®.

"Sheesh, will you lighten up?" said Dad. He took another swig of his ExtraFoamyRootbeer®. "All I'm saying is that when I was a young man I was always punchin' and kickin' and scrapin' and stealin' and chewin' and bitin' and rollin' and toilet-paperin' and tumblin' and spittin' and cow-tippin' and rock-tossin' and . . ." Dad went on like this for a solid two minutes, then passed out face-first in his Potatoes'N'Peas'N'Ham®.

I didn't think my siblings would take Dad's comment seriously. We'd all agreed he was overworked as a mailman—stressed by a recent uptick in ThoughtfulThankYouNotes®—and that his comments were best PolitelyIgnored®. But then, a week later, my youngest brothers pedaled their ShinyRedTenSpeeds® to the house of our old piano teacher and heaved a rock through one of her DelicateLaceCurtainedWindows®.

My brothers were apprehended immediately—taken down to the police station in a blur of FourthOfJulyColors®. I stayed up all night worrying. It seemed plausible that my family's time in Delight® would end. What would happen to Dad, his blood pressure? What would happen to all of us? The news I'd meant to share at dinner was that my wife and I had a baby on the way. We had already picked out a Reputable® name—George® for a boy, Georgina® for a girl—and stocked the nursery with FunButEducationalToys®. And yet here was my Dad, giving un-Reputable® advice. Here were my siblings making un-Reputable® choices. All night I paced back and forth on the front porch of my CuteCouple'sCottage®, waking up the neighborhood dogs with my worrying.

At dawn, I heard that my brothers had only been charged with BoysWillBeBoys®.

They came out of the constable's office grinning and blushing. By afternoon they were at our piano teacher's house, making repairs on the window while she serenaded them with OldTimeyTunes®. Afterward they all ate biscuits and ChuckledOverHonestMistakes®.

Life seemed to be back to normal, but I couldn't shake the feeling that my family had almost lost AReallyGoodThing®—maybe TheBestThingAPersonCouldHave®—and that we could still lose it. My work as a crossing guard suffered. More than one fellow townsperson tapped me on the shoulder to correct a drooping WaitForWalkers® sign, the embarrassment of which made me feel decidedly un-Splendidly®.

My wife suffered too. She offered fewer cheers whenever I mowed the lawn or washed the car. Instead she looked down at her belly, rubbed the small hillock that was George®/Georgina®. My heart raced when she did this. I wanted to protect that child. I wanted to give George®/Georgina® TheBestThingAPersonCouldHave®.

I decided to confront Dad about how he was behaving Friendshipful® toward the Ne'er-Do-Wells, and to explain why this was un-Friendshipful® toward his neighbors and his family in Delight®. I developed stern but loving arguments, practicing them in front of the bathroom mirror, then again in front of my wife, who managed a short yet Tender'N'Inspirational® cheer. As I walked from my house to his house, I felt Happily-Hopeful®. I even whistled some OldTimeyTunes®, picturing Dad and me ChucklingOverHonestMistakes®. And then the two of us engaging in a TenderHug®.

What I discovered at Dad's house, however, was decidedly un-Pleasantness®. On the front porch sprawled a hodgepodge group of individuals. Some of them were drinking ExtraFoamy-Rootbeer®, then tossing the empty cans up on the roof. Others walked in and out of the house without removing their boots. These were big bearded fellows who, when I addressed them, did not follow ProperHandshakeProtocol® (too firm, too sweaty, too many pumps). There were women as well: women who spat on the ground and who did not seem to care whether doors were held open for them. Women with un-PoliteTableTalk® images tattooed on their arms. And in the middle of all these Ne'er-Do-Wells sat Dad, strumming an un-Reputable® musical instrument. He was laughing with a gap-toothed man.

"Son!" called Dad, seeing me. "Come meet my buddy Gap-Tooth."

You could say that at that moment I had a vision. I saw Delight®, but a different Delight®. I saw a Delight® that was overcrowded and subdivided and littered. A Delight® that had dissolved into the grim commonness of everywhere else. At first, as more outsiders arrived, the changes would seem harmless. We would run out of flavors at the IceCreamJamboree®, blankets during the Sunset-Picnics®. But then there wouldn't be enough spots for everyone to play on the baseball team. Or parts in the school band. Or jobs as crossing guards, postal workers, or floral arrangement consultants. Residents would become un-Contented®. More rocks would be thrown through more DelicateLaceCurtainedWindows®. And once that kind of crime began, what was next? To be Warmly-Welcoming® to strangers in Delight® meant being Warmly-Welcoming® to our own demise.

So if we're being TotallyTruthful®, it was me who called the constable over to Dad's house. It was me who watched the Ne'er-

Do-Wells get carted away in a blur of FourthOfJulyColors®, Dad among them.

"What happened after the explosion in the French cheese factory?" Dad yelled out the car window, but I pretended not to hear. I didn't even wave.

When my siblings discovered what had happened, all of us were filled with different emotions—GoodNaturedConfusion®, Jubilance®, Jubilance®, JustifiableChagrin®, FlutteringStomach-Butterflies®—but eventually we agreed it was for the best. Dad had acted like a Dad, not a Dad®. And for little George®/Georgina®, he certainly wouldn't have been much of a Granddad®.

Even with him and the Ne'er-Do-Wells gone, however, I still didn't feel that my family was totally safe. So at Delight's® annual TalkativeTownAssembly®, I proposed the idea of a BigWhite-PicketFence®. Everyone agreed it was a Splendidly® idea. We had the thing built in less than a month, all of the town's residents chipping in, whether by hammering nails or carrying plywood or baking BerryliciousCrumbles® for afternoon snacks.

And the fence, when it was finished, was AReallyGoodThing®. It wrapped all the way around Delight®, sealing our borders and protecting our Bright'N'ShiningFuture®. It's a point of pride for everyone now: this wall that is too thick punch through, too deep to tunnel under, and, most importantly, TooTallToSeeOut®.

Americans

on

Mars!

————————————
▬▬▬▬▬▬▬

1.

What they don't tell you—but you learn soon enough—is that you can't cry in space. There's no gravity to pull tears down. They just stay put, puddled in your eyes.

You can't get an erection either. But that's more on account of the in-flight spacesuit/hyperbaric chamber.

2.

There are twenty-two other colonists aboard the ship—including me and my lady, Tanya. We're part of a pilot program to up numbers at the American base. The other colonists are all "paragons of intelligence, patriotism, moral fortitude, and personal hygiene."

All of them think I also fit those criteria.

If my brothers were here, they'd tell me I was rolling with a bunch of dweebs. My brothers took great pride in being idiots—can-crushing, glue-inhaling, TV-stealing, flea-rearing fuck-ups—and until eight months ago, I took great pride in that too.

Tanya looks over at me from her spacesuit/hyperbaric chamber. "Almost there," she mouths, her lips floating open and closed like two red feathers.

3.

When our spaceship penetrates the exosphere, everyone puts on extra seat belts. The fuselage groans, air shafts squealing, control panels woozy with lights. I close my eyes and imagine being vaporized in a giant, terrible explosion. It's actually kind of comforting, the idea: like getting permanently blackout drunk and staggering guiltless, joyful, around the universe.

The groaning and squealing stops.

I open my eyes and see that the others have flung off their seat belts—they're embracing and whooping, some of them crying—because gravity is back, so they can.

Tanya winks at me, like we've just pulled off a prank.

I suppose, in a way, we have.

I feel dumb for imagining the explosion.

"Come 'ere," murmurs Tanya, and we kiss like a couple who've been kissing for years, who've been screwing for years, who aren't just two strangers who met on accident, eight months ago, and decided to make a stab at the impossible (one in a thousand, our application odds). We kiss for over a minute. We kiss until we aren't just kissing to fool the others, we're kissing to fool ourselves, and when we do finally stop, neither of us knows what to say, other than "Holyshit-fuck," because, "Goddamn," we survived the trip—avoided asteroids and cosmic rays and Extremely Thorough Background Checks—because we, of all people, get to start a new life.

4.

Before arriving on Mars, I tried picturing how the colony would look. All I could picture, though, were scenes from movies. Giant geodesic igloos. Doors that hissed when they opened. Hovercrafts racing across dusty red plains.

Turns out Mars looks exactly like the movies.

"Welcome, welcome, welcome," says a woman with teeth as polar-white as her lab coat. She smiles at all of us newcomers—freshly oxygenated, vitaminized, sanitized, handshooked, hugged—as we file into an auditorium. "Long flight?" asks the woman, the first in a string of unfunny jokes that everyone har-hars at anyway. But then she also says serious things. She talks about the situation back on Earth: about preemptive crisis aversion, auxiliary demographics, and the great work we are doing for our country—hell, our species. Her words make me sit up straight. I hadn't thought much about what I was doing on Mars, only how to get there. But then Tanya squeezes my hand, and I remember that while she may have forged most of my papers—including our marriage certificate, an IQ test, and a gold-standard genome map—my fertility ratings were authentically off the charts.

"You all have a lot of work ahead of you," says the white-toothed lady beaming at all of us couples, equations of 1+1. "You might as well get started."

More har-harring.

I look over at Tanya, who's chewing on the end of her dark braid, like she's concentrating real hard. I know what she's probably thinking. I'm thinking it too: Tanya and I haven't actually done it yet. It's not that we don't have chemistry. Tanya's got some Puerto Rican in her, so she always looks tan, and me, I've had biceps since I was fourteen—but back on Earth we didn't have much time to get to know one another. And then it was Tanya's idea to "make it special." She really did want a fresh start. And while I'd been kind of annoyed, I also kind of respected her.

Really, I did.

Eight months, though, is a long time to wait. So when the meeting ends, I'm plenty glad to carry Tanya across the threshold of our couple-sized igloo, to lay her down on our couple-sized sleep pod, to see her grin, her dark hair spilling oil slick everywhere, to feel blood charge through my veins.

I can't, however, seem to get hard.

"Hey, Rex?" says Tanya, knocking on the bathroom door, where I've retreated to buy some time. Under other circumstances, I might have admired the bathroom's gadgety chrome cleanness. Instead, I'm panicking. I'm panicking because this has never happened before—or, more specifically, never not happened. "You ready?" says Tanya, in a way that's meant to sound coy, but that's also all business.

I try imagining Tanya beckoning me into bed—Tanya, peeling off her shirt, the warm press of her skin—Tanya, doing unmentionable things.

Nothing.

"I need a little space right now," I yell through the bathroom door, which is something I've never ever ever ever ever said to a woman trying to get me into bed.

5.

I say this to her the next day. And then the next.

6.

"Faggot." That's what my brothers would've called me. If they were here, they would've gut-punched me windless, beat me till I puked up my lunch, spit teeth. Then they'd piss on me as I lay in a black-eyed, bleeding heap.

Picturing this, I almost miss them.

"You serious?" my brothers would have said, if they'd seen Tanya. "I'd sell my left nut for a night with that chick!"

I owe Tanya too. She got me into the space program in the first place. A real smart girl. We met in a refugee camp for people from Florida, because—while I'm not from Florida—I was always in the market for a free meal. Tanya was in the market for a husband. "You ever get a girl pregnant?" she asked, straight up, after catching me ogling her from the grub line. I had assumed she was a nutcase. She was a lot dirtier then, her eyes like little birds, darting all over. Even so, I told her that I had. I was nineteen and kind of proud of it. "The girl keep your baby?" she asked. I shook my head, unexpectedly ashamed. I asked what the hell she wanted. Having lost my place in the grub line, I was extra annoyed. But then Tanya's eyes stilled, got sparkly. She told me about the space program, the chance to start a new life—a good life, an easy life—and that she'd been looking for someone like me. "Someone like who?" I asked. Tanya gave me an up-down, same as I'd given her a moment before. "Someone," she said, "with no ties to this world."

7.
Couples that are already pregnant:
June & Alfonso
Spirit & Rusty

They're nice people, the other colonists. Accomplished people. Spirit, for instance, was a chess champion on Earth, and Rusty some kind of big-shot sculptor. You'd think they'd want to talk about something other than babies. But it's just babies, all day long: egg sacks and zygotes and in-utero Springsteen concerts ("It excels cognitive development up to twenty percent!"). Even Mark, a beefy, mustached, former Olympic swimmer, only wanted to discuss ovulation patterns.

And Tanya? I've been avoiding her mostly.

Today, though, I met Felipé—whose wife isn't pregnant yet either. We ate lunch in the cafeteria, and he told me all about his thrilling life as a scholar of American Exceptionalism.

Actually, Felipé was kind of a dweeb. For a moment, I couldn't help picturing my brothers beating the shit out of him: biting his wire spectacles in half, slamming him over the head with his own thesaurus. Stifling a laugh, I nearly choked on my grilled cheese.

"Are you unwell?" Felipé peered at me as if I were fine print. "Shall I solicit help?"

I shook my head, still coughing up bits of sandwich. I'd noticed the white-toothed lady and her entourage of scientists enter the cafeteria. They looked right at me—all of them—looked with some intensity. Did they know I hadn't been sleeping with Tanya? Could they tell? And, if so, would they revisit my files, ask questions, poke around? And what if I turned out to not only be dead weight, but lying, cheating, illegal dead weight? They couldn't send me back, that was part of the whole deal. There wasn't the technology yet for return trips. What would they do? Would there be some sort of Soylent Green scenario—would I get liquefied for food?

I fled the cafeteria. Felipé came too, fluttering along behind me, having announced, "A post-lunch constitutional sounds splendid." I didn't have a particular destination in mind, so together we wandered through the colony's tubular hallways, passing various igloos—the Greenhouse, the Mineral Lab, Waste Treatment, et cetera—both of us greeting the other colonists we passed along the way. By the time we got to the Rec Room, I was feeling much better. Tanya and I, we'd figure things out. And the white-toothed lady? Whatever. Felipé and I played a few rounds of ping-pong against some astrophysicists, then flopped down among the bean-bag chairs on the observation deck. Someone put on a funky jam—dweeb music, nothing I'd ever heard before—but I still kind of liked it. *What a life,* I couldn't help thinking. *What a goddamn good life!*

Outside, a rust-red wind swirled across a rocky plain, coating the metal carcasses of a few early Mars Rovers. Speared in the dirt, an American flag twitched and quivered.

"You know," said Felipé, "I'm from Arizona, so this feels just like home."

His mention of home punctured my good mood. Even with Felipé smiling at me, all I could picture was the old shipping container where my brothers and I had lived. The rankness and muck and the knives we'd kept under our pillows.

It didn't help, either, that then Tanya walked by, arm in arm with some of the other wives, frowning at me.

"*Women,*" I said to Felipé, trying to act casual. "Am I right?"

"Indeed," replied Felipé. "They love reminding us how expendable we are!" He chuckled, as if this was funny, then jiggled forward in his beanbag, pushing his spectacles up the bridge of his nose. "That reminds me," he said. "I'm organizing a Thanksgiving Day Pageant—I know, I know, why have a pageant when there aren't any young ones here? Well, some of us thought it would be a good to practice. They'll be here soon enough!"

He pinched my cheek, his thumb and forefinger surprisingly hard.

8.

Whitney & Mark
Fatima & Sebastian
Lorraine & Ezekiel

9.

"How are you feeling?" says Tanya. Usually she's asleep by the time I slip back into our igloo. But tonight she's stayed up waiting—wearing a tight Lycra suit—so she's all breasts and hips and ass. "I'm kinda tired," I tell her, nodding at the igloo porthole: Mars's multiple moons suspended in the sky. Tanya snorts, her nostrils flaring. "Really, Rex? That's all you got to say for yourself?" She sucks in air. "Look, we don't need to be in love, we just—"

Even when Tanya's wearing her Lycra suit, her hair done up in a sleek bun, I can still see the dirt-smudged girl I first met: the girl with scavenging eyes, clawing her way toward a better life.

I feel kinda bad, but also riled up—because Tanya could be a little more understanding. "Cut me come slack," I say. "I'm under a lot of pressure."

Tanya doesn't look too impressed. "*You're* under a lot of pressure?" Her voice is soft but cold. "I am not going to let you screw this up for me."

It takes a minute to process what she means, but once I do, I must look upset, because then Tanya tries to backtrack. She tells me she wants to make this work—she's trying to make this work—and that I understand her in a way no one else in the colony can. That no one else ever will. This makes me I wonder if she feels lonely too: alone with a skin-toothed past she has to keep hidden.

Tanya insists that I see a doctor.

I want to explain to her that my condition might not be a physical problem so much as a psychosomatic-existential one—but since I'm kind of an idiot, I can't quite get the words out.

10.

Carolina & Ferdinand
Daisy & Walt
Petra & Mark

11.

The space station doctor is a broad-shouldered man with a face out of a razor commercial; a man with an easy laugh and photos of golden retrievers all over his office.

I dislike him immediately.

"Well," says the Doc, after poking and measuring and staring at me. "Everything looks shipshape. You just wanted a checkup? Was there anything specific you wanted to discuss?" He pulls up a stool and sits down beside me. He even smells nice: like toothpaste and leather. "How's life on Mars been treating you?"

The honest answer? Good. Life on Mars was better than I ever could have imagined. I got all the grilled cheese sandwiches I wanted. I had twenty-four-hour access to a fitness center, cable TV, and geothermal hot springs. No one ever called me Fucktard or Fag-Face or tried to steal my shoes. People of all races and religions lived together in a fully operational representative democracy. And from what I've heard, Mars also had excellent "biostability." When's the last time someone said that about Earth? The other day I saw a news report from Washington: "Heat Wave Continues," "Walmart Layoffs Continue," "Food Shortages Continue," "Riots Increasing."

"Son?" says the Doc. "What's troubling you?"

I want to like this man. I want to confide in him, to have him pat my back and tell me I'm doing my best. But how could I explain that every time I feel the slightest procreative urge, I make a guilty spiral back toward Earth, toward the humid swill, the hungriness and long lines and everyone walking around coughing and scared? That I picture my brothers stealing food and huffing solvents to get by?

And anyway, what could he do?

12.

Felipé and his lady are pregnant.

I ask if he wants to go smash something to celebrate. That's what my brothers and I always did.

"Ha ha," he says, "you're a funny one, Rex."

13.

Want to know something actually funny? I don't think I was even related to any of my brothers, since FrankenFace and Timeole were Asian, and Spit-Finger Deluxe was albino. But we bloodied one another so often that a little bit of each of us must have mixed in with a little bit of everyone else.

Even funnier? When I told my brothers I was leaving—that I'd got myself a girl and a one-way ticket to paradise—FrankenFace, drunk on paint thinner, cuffed me around the ear and said, "You're just gonna bail on us, you fucking piece of shit?" And I'd looked over his shoulder, into the shipping container where Spit-Finger Deluxe and RhinoSpaz were swinging a rat around by its tail, and everyone else was getting high on aerosol spray cans—Timeole lying spread eagle, his nose a bright shade of blue.

"Bail on what?" I'd answered. Then I turned and left without looking back.

14.

Tanya and I are the only unimpregnated couple.

"It's not that big a deal," I tell her. "Who wants to follow the crowd?"

Tanya looks at me like I'm the biggest bonehead-dweeb-fuck-up in the solar system. "Don't even talk to me," she says. "Just get away from me."

For about thirty seconds I feel relieved—like the pressure's finally off—then I feel ten times worse.

15.

The thing I dislike most about a Mars day? It's 2.7 percent longer than an Earth day. That's 2.7 percent longer to fumble about, not performing my one damn responsibility, 2.7 percent longer to avoid the administrators, 2.7 percent longer to pretend you are an upstanding citizen. It might not sound like much, but trust me, it is.

16.

I work up the courage to talk to Tanya again, this time for real. She's still in our igloo when I find her, sitting on our sleep pod. "Hey," I say. She doesn't look up. "Hey," I try again, "I was thinking—"

Then I see that she's crying, tears streaking her face in a shimmering veil.

I start feeling very far away—like I'm floating on the ceiling or in the sky—like I'm watching myself hardly know anything about this woman but still mess up her life real bad.

I can't seem to say anything, though. I can't even reach out to touch her.

Then, a knock on our igloo door. I peer through the peephole and see the white-toothed lady, flanked by two buff spectrologists, pens behind their ears like javelins. "Rex," says the lady, "We need—"

The door hisses open. I push past them and scurry down the hallway like a hamster with nowhere to hide. I break left, then right, stalling in the Rec Room. I begin seriously considering stealing one of the hovercrafts and escaping into Martian wilderness.

But, really, how long could I last?

A hand thumps my shoulder. It's Felipé. I'm so grateful to see a friend that I actually hug him. Felipé seems excited as well. "I'm simply ecstatic you're here," he says. "We're about to start practicing for the Thanksgiving Pageant—you mind holding this?" He hands me a glue stick. Two colonists approach, carrying a large cardboard ship. Felipé whistles, as if he's seeing a hot piece of ass. "What a beauty," he says. "May I?" Before I know it, the other colonists have lifted the ship over my head and I'm standing in the middle, two shoulder straps holding it off the ground. "You make a damn fine Mayflower," Felipé says, rubbing his hands. "Now, what was it you were asking?"

I hadn't asked anything, but I figure this might be my last opportunity to shed light on some issues. "Hey, man," I say, "you ever think about all those people who—hypothetically—might have deserved to be up here instead of you? Like maybe your neighbors? Or your friends?" I try to act casual, like I'm just being intellectual or something. "Or your brothers?"

Felipé pushes his glasses up the bridge of his nose. "Well, you see, my boy." He tugs at my costume, beaming as other colonists start filtering in for the pageant. "It's good for everyone, us being here. Good for our country's morale . . ."

He keeps talking, but I can't concentrate because, right then, I notice that Tanya's arrived. She's wiped her face clean, braided her hair, and put on a beige-colored sack. She's dressed up like the prettiest Pocahontas on the whole planet.

". . . Which brings us back to Frederick Jackson Turner," continues Felipé. "The Frontier Thesis! It's important for our nation's people to feel like there's room to dream . . ."

Tanya sees me, then turns away. She starts talking to a few of the other colonists, some of whom are costumed as pilgrims, one as a turkey, along with a few stalks of corn and other vegetables. She giggles, giving the the Turkey Guy a little shove. I feel all hot and trembly with jealousy. I've been telling myself that she wouldn't sleep with other men—but, really, what allegiance would she have?

"Manifest Destiny!" exclaims Felipé, but all I can think is, *Why did Tanya even pick me? Why me, of all people?*

The question makes me feel claustrophobic, itchy. I start trying to extract myself from the cardboard Mayflower, but Felipé notices and says, "Hold steady. I just got it right." Then some of the other colonists come over—the Turkey Guy and someone dressed as a potato. "You think of any baby names yet?" the Turkey Guy asks Felipé. "Oh yes," Felipé answers, "Kiki has a whole list. We were thinking something classic, iconic. Hillary or Oprah if it's a girl. Shaquille or Ronald if it's a boy."

"Wonderful, wonderful," says the Potato.

"How about you Rex?" says the Turkey Guy, "You and Tanya been thinking of baby names?"

I can't hold it together any longer. I fling the glue stick I'm holding against the wall. Everyone turns. Stares at me. "Oh my," says Felipé, adjusting his glasses. I start trying to get the cardboard Mayflower off, but it turns out to be very well constructed, so I ram it against a wall-side control panel. The lights flicker and hum. Everyone looks at me with polite distress, some of the pilgrim women covering their mouths. "Son?" says the Turkey Guy, who I realize is actually the doctor. I punch him in the face—my hand hurts, but it feels damn good. I tear the "Welcome to America" sign off the wall. I jump up and down on the fake fire pit. I laugh, imagining that somewhere my brothers are laughing with me. I imagine them looking up into the sky and cheering me on. Now people are getting genuinely agitated—someone's buzzing the administrators—everyone, I notice, except Tanya. She's standing in the corner half smiling. Like she's proud of me. Like she's been waiting for this all along. I grin back like a maniac and rip myself free of the cardboard ship. Maybe I even beat my chest. Maybe I throw a basket of colored feathers up into the air so that they rain down like flock of settling birds.

Tanya beckons. I go to her. My body seems to swell, to fill the whole room—hell, the whole planet. "That's him," I hear someone say, then the thump of running footsteps, the electric hum of Tasers. I grab Tanya's hand and squeeze. She squeezes back, her eyes opening up huge—like a bottomless lake or a starless sky— like a future, thick with unknowables, still waiting to be made.

THE IOWA SHORT FICTION AWARD AND THE JOHN SIMMONS
SHORT FICTION AWARD WINNERS, 1970–2016

Donald Anderson
Fire Road
Dianne Benedict
Shiny Objects
Marie-Helene Bertino
Safe as Houses
Will Boast
Power Ballads
David Borofka
Hints of His Mortality
Robert Boswell
Dancing in the Movies
Mark Brazaitis
*The River of Lost Voices:
Stories from Guatemala*
Jack Cady
The Burning and Other Stories
Pat Carr
The Women in the Mirror
Kathryn Chetkovich
Friendly Fire
Cyrus Colter
The Beach Umbrella
Jennine Capó Crucet
How to Leave Hialeah
Jennifer S. Davis
Her Kind of Want
Janet Desaulniers
What You've Been Missing
Sharon Dilworth
The Long White
Susan M. Dodd
Old Wives' Tales
Merrill Feitell
*Here Beneath Low-Flying
Planes*
James Fetler
Impossible Appetites
Starkey Flythe, Jr.
Lent: The Slow Fast
Kathleen Founds
*When Mystical Creatures
Attack!*

Sohrab Homi Fracis
*Ticket to Minto: Stories of
India and America*
H. E. Francis
The Itinerary of Beggars
Abby Frucht
Fruit of the Month
Tereze Glück
*May You Live in Interesting
Times*
Ivy Goodman
Heart Failure
Barbara Hamby
Lester Higata's 20th Century
Edward Hamlin
*Night in Erg Chebbi and Other
Stories*
Ann Harleman
Happiness
Elizabeth Harris
The Ant Generator
Ryan Harty
Bring Me Your Saddest Arizona
Charles Haverty
Excommunicados
Mary Hedin
Fly Away Home
Beth Helms
American Wives
Jim Henry
*Thank You for Being
Concerned and Sensitive*
Allegra Hyde
Of This New World
Lisa Lenzo
Within the Lighted City
Kathryn Ma
*All That Work and Still No
Boys*
Renée Manfredi
Where Love Leaves Us
Susan Onthank Mates
The Good Doctor